Ian Livingstone

DEATHTRAP DUNGEON

Illustrated by Iain McCaig

Puffin Books

Puffin Books, Penguin Books Ltd, Harmondsworth, Middlesex, England
Penguin Books, 40 West 23rd Street, New York, New York 10010, U.S.A.
Penguin Books Australia Ltd, Ringwood, Victoria, Australia
Penguin Books Canada Ltd, 2801 John Street, Markham, Ontario, Canada L3R 1B4
Penguin Books (N.Z.) Ltd, 182–190 Wairau Road, Auckland 10, New Zealand

First published 1984
Reprinted 1984

Printed and bound in Great Britain by
Cox & Wyman Ltd, Reading
Set in 11/13 pt Linotron Palatino by
Rowland Phototypesetting Ltd
Bury St Edmunds, Suffolk

DATE DUE

Down in the dark, twisting labyrinth of Fang, unknown horrors await you. Devised by the devilish mind of Baron Sukumvit, the labyrinth is riddled with fiendish traps and bloodthirsty monsters, which will test your skills almost beyond the limit of endurance. Countless adventurers before you have taken up the challenge of the Trial of Champions and walked through the carved mouth of the labyrinth, never to be seen again. Do YOU dare enter?

Tempted by the promise of a fabulous prize – and the lure of the unbeaten challenge – YOU are one of six seasoned fighters prepared to take on the labyrinth. Only one of you may win through – the rest will perish. But which of you will it be?

Two dice, a pencil and an eraser are all you need to embark on this thrilling adventure of sword and sorcery, complete with its elaborate combat system and a score sheet to record your gains and losses.

Many dangers lie ahead and your success is by no means certain. Powerful adversaries are ranged against you and often your only choice is to kill or be killed!

Other Fighting Fantasy Gamebooks published in Puffin are: *The Warlock of Firetop Mountain*, *The Citadel of Chaos*, *The Forest of Doom*, *Starship Traveller*, *City of Thieves* and *Island of the Lizard King*.

For Jacques and Octavie Gelaude

CONTENTS

HOW TO FIGHT THE CREATURES OF DEATHTRAP DUNGEON

Before embarking on your adventure, you must first determine your own strengths and weaknesses. You have in your possession a sword and a backpack containing provisions (food and drink) for the trip. You have been preparing for your quest by training yourself in swordplay and exercising vigorously to build up your stamina.

To see how effective your preparations have been you must use the dice to determine your initial SKILL and STAMINA scores. On pages 18–19 there is an *Adventure Sheet* which you may use to record the details of an adventure. On it you will find boxes for recording your SKILL and STAMINA scores.

You are advised to either record your scores on the *Adventure Sheet* in pencil, or make photocopies of the page to use in future adventures.

Skill, Stamina and Luck

Roll one die. Add 6 to this number and enter this total in the SKILL box on the *Adventure Sheet*.

Roll both dice. Add 12 to the number rolled and enter this total in the STAMINA box.

There is also a LUCK box. Roll one die, add 6 to this number and enter this total in the LUCK box.

For reasons that will be explained below, SKILL, STAMINA and LUCK scores change constantly during an adventure. You must keep an accurate record of these scores and for this reason you are advised either to write small in the boxes or to keep an eraser handy. But never rub out your *Initial* scores. Although you may be awarded additional SKILL, STAMINA and LUCK points, these totals may never exceed your *Initial* scores, except on very rare occasions, when you will be instructed on a particular page.

Your SKILL score reflects your swordsmanship and general fighting expertise; the higher the better. Your STAMINA score reflects your general constitution, your will to survive, your determination and overall fitness; the higher your STAMINA score, the longer you will be able to survive. Your LUCK score indicates how naturally lucky a person you are. Luck – and magic – are facts of life in the fantasy kingdom you are about to explore.

Battles

You will often come across pages in the book which instruct you to fight a creature of some sort. An option to flee may be given, but if not – or if you choose to attack the creature anyway – you must resolve the battle as described below.

First record the creature's SKILL and STAMINA scores in the first vacant Monster Encounter Box on your *Adventure Sheet*. The scores for each creature are given in the book each time you have an encounter.

The sequence of combat is then:

1. Roll both dice once for the creature. Add its SKILL score. This total is the creature's Attack Strength.

2. Roll both dice once for yourself. Add the number rolled to your current SKILL score. This total is your Attack Strength.

3. If your Attack Strength is higher than that of the creature, you have wounded it. Proceed to step 4. If the creature's Attack Strength is higher than yours, it has wounded you. Proceed to step 5. If both Attack Strength totals are the same, you have avoided each other's blows – start the next Attack Round from step 1 above.

4. You have wounded the creature, so subtract 2 points from its STAMINA score. You may use your LUCK here to do additional damage (see over).

5. The creature has wounded you, so subtract 2 points from your own STAMINA score. Again you may use LUCK at this stage (see over).

6. Make the appropriate adjustments to either the creature's or your own STAMINA scores (and your LUCK score if you used LUCK – see over).

7. Begin the next Attack Round by returning to your current SKILL score and repeating steps

1–6. This sequence continues until the STAMINA score of either you or the creature you are fighting has been reduced to zero (death).

Escaping

On some pages you may be given the option of running away from a battle should things be going badly for you. However, if you do run away, the creature automatically gets in one wound on you (subtract 2 STAMINA points) as you flee. Such is the price of cowardice. Note that you may use LUCK on this wound in the normal way (see below). You may only *Escape* if that option is specifically given to you on the page.

Fighting More Than One Creature

If you come across more than one creature in a particular encounter, the instructions on that page will tell you how to handle the battle. Sometimes you will treat them as a single monster; sometimes you will fight each one in turn.

Luck

At various times during your adventure, either in battles or when you come across situations in which you could either be lucky or unlucky (details of these are given on the pages themselves), you may call on your luck to make the outcome more favourable. But beware! Using luck is a risky business and if you are *un*lucky, the results could be disastrous.

The procedure for using your luck is as follows: roll two dice. If the number rolled is equal to or less than your current LUCK score, you have been lucky and the result will go in your favour. If the number rolled is higher than your current LUCK score, you have been unlucky and you will be penalized.

This procedure is known as *Testing your Luck*. Each time you *Test your Luck*, you must subtract one point from your current LUCK score. Thus you will soon realize that the more you rely on your luck, the more risky this will become.

Using Luck in Battles

On certain pages of the book you will be told to *Test your Luck* and will be told the consequences of your being lucky or unlucky. However, in battles, you always have the option of using your luck either to inflict a more serious wound on a creature you have just wounded, or to minimize the effects of a wound the creature has just inflicted on you.

If you have just wounded the creature, you may *Test your Luck* as described above. If you are lucky, you have inflicted a severe wound and may subtract an *extra* 2 points from the creature's STAMINA score. However, if you are unlucky, the wound was a mere graze and you must restore 1 point to the creature's STAMINA (i.e. instead of scoring the normal 2 points of damage, you have now scored only 1).

If the creature has just wounded you, you may *Test your Luck* to try to minimize the wound. If you are lucky, you have managed to avoid the full damage of the blow. Restore 1 point of STAMINA (i.e. instead of doing 2 points of damage it has done only 1). If you are unlucky, you have taken a more serious blow. Subtract 1 extra STAMINA point.

Remember that you must subtract 1 point from your own LUCK score each time you *Test your Luck*.

Restoring Skill, Stamina and Luck

Skill

Your SKILL score will not change much during your adventure. Occasionally, a page may give instructions to increase or decrease your SKILL score. A Magic Weapon may increase your SKILL, but remember that only one weapon can be used at a time! You cannot claim 2 SKILL bonuses for carrying two Magic Swords. Your SKILL score can never exceed its *Initial* value unless specifically instructed. Drinking the Potion of Skill (see later) will restore your SKILL to its *Initial* level at any time.

Stamina and Provisions

Your STAMINA score will change a lot during your adventure as you fight monsters and undertake arduous tasks. As you near your goal, your STAMINA level may be dangerously low and battles may be particularly risky, so be careful!

Your backpack contains enough Provisions for ten meals. You may rest and eat at any time except when engaged in a Battle. Eating a meal restores 4 STAMINA points. When you eat a meal, add 4 points to your STAMINA score and deduct 1 point from your Provisions. A separate Provisions Remaining box is provided on the *Adventure Sheet* for recording details of Provisions. Remember that you have a long way to go, so use your Provisions wisely!

Remember also that your STAMINA score may never exceed its *Initial* value unless specifically instructed on a page. Drinking the Potion of Strength (see later) will restore your STAMINA to its *Initial* level at any time.

Luck

Additions to your LUCK score are awarded through the adventure when you have been particularly lucky. Details are given on the pages of the book. Remember that, as with SKILL and STAMINA, your LUCK score may never exceed its *Initial* value unless specifically instructed on a page. Drinking the Potion of Fortune (see later) will restore your LUCK to its *Initial* level at any time, and increase your *Initial* LUCK by 1 point.

EQUIPMENT AND POTIONS

You will start your adventure with a bare minimum of equipment, but you may find or buy other items during your travels. You are armed with a sword and are dressed in leather armour. You have a backpack to hold your Provisions and any treasures you may come across.

In addition, you may take one bottle of a magical potion which will aid you on your quest. You may choose to take a bottle of any of the following:

A Potion of Skill – restores SKILL points
A Potion of Strength – restores STAMINA points
A Potion of Fortune – restores LUCK points and adds 1 to *Initial* LUCK

These potions may be taken at any time during your adventure (except when engaged in a Battle). Taking a measure of potion will restore SKILL, STAMINA or LUCK scores to their *Initial* level (and the Potion of Fortune will add 1 point to your *Initial* LUCK score before LUCK is restored).

Each bottle of potion contains enough for *one* measure, i.e. the characteristic may be restored once during an adventure. Make a note on your *Adventure Sheet* when you have used up a potion.

Remember also that you may only choose *one* of the three potions to take on your trip, so choose wisely!

HINTS ON PLAY

There is one true way through Deathtrap Dungeon and it will take you several attempts to find it. Make notes and draw a map as you explore – this map will be invaluable in future adventures and enable you to progress rapidly through to unexplored sections.

Not all areas contain treasure; many merely contain traps and creatures which you will no doubt fall foul of. There are many 'wild-goose chase' passages and while you may indeed progress through to your ultimate destination, it is by no means certain that you will find what you are searching for.

It will be realized that entries make no sense if read in numerical order. It is essential that you read only the entries you are instructed to read. Reading other entries will only cause confusion and may lessen the excitement during play.

The one true way involves a minimum of risk and any player, no matter how weak on initial dice rolls, should be able to get through fairly easily.

May the luck of the gods go with you on the adventure ahead!

ADVENTURE SHEET

SKILL	STAMINA	LUCK
Initial	*Initial*	*Initial*
Skill =	*Stamina =*	*Luck =*

ITEMS OF EQUIPMENT CARRIED

GOLD

JEWELS

POTIONS

PROVISIONS REMAINING

MONSTER ENCOUNTER BOXES

Skill = *Stamina =*	*Skill =* *Stamina =*	*Skill =* *Stamina =*
Skill = *Stamina =*	*Skill =* *Stamina =*	*Skill =* *Stamina =*
Skill = *Stamina =*	*Skill =* *Stamina =*	*Skill =* *Stamina =*
Skill = *Stamina =*	*Skill =* *Stamina =*	*Skill =* *Stamina =*

BACKGROUND

Despite its name, Fang was an ordinary small town in the northern province of Chiang Mai. Situated on the banks of the River Kok it made a convenient stopover for river traders and passengers throughout most of the year. A few barges, rafts and sometimes even a large sailboat could usually be found moored at Fang. But all that was long ago, before the creation of the Trial of Champions. Now once a year the river is crammed with boats as people arrive from hundreds of miles around, hoping to witness the breaking of an ancient tradition in Fang and see a victor in the Trial of Champions.

On 1 May each year, warriors and heroes come to Fang to face the test of their lives. Survival is unlikely, yet many take the risk, for the prize is great – a purse of 10,000 Gold Pieces and the freedom of Chiang Mai forever. However, to become Champion is no easy task. Some years ago, a powerful baron of Fang called Sukumvit decided to bring attention to his town by creating the ultimate contest. With the help of the townspeople, he constructed a labyrinth deep in the hillside behind Fang, from which there was only one exit. The labyrinth was filled with all kinds of deadly tricks and traps and loathsome monsters. Sukumvit had designed it in meticulous detail so that anybody hoping to face its challenge would have to use their wits as well as weaponskill. When he was finally satisfied that all was complete, he put his labyrinth to the test. He picked ten of his finest guards and, fully armed, they marched into the labyrinth. They were never seen again. The tale of the ill-fated guards soon spread throughout the land, and it was then that Sukumvit announced the first Trial of Champions. Messengers and news-sheets carried his challenge – 10,000 Gold Pieces and the freedom of Chiang Mai forever to any person surviving the perils of the labyrinth of Fang. The first year, seventeen brave warriors attempted 'The Walk', as it later came to be known. Not one reappeared. As the years passed and the Trial of Champions continued, it attracted more and more challengers and spectators. Fang prospered and would prepare itself months in advance for the spectacle it hosted each May. The town would be decorated, tents erected, dining-halls built, musicians, dancers, fire-eaters, illusionists and every sort of entertainer hired, and entries registered from hopeful individuals intent on making 'The Walk'. The last week of April found the people of Fang and its visitors in wild celebration. Everybody sang, drank, danced and laughed until day broke on 1 May, when the town thronged to the gates of the labyrinth to watch the first challenger of the year step forward to face the Trial of Champions.

Having seen one of Sukumvit's challenges nailed to a tree, you decide that this year you will attempt 'The Walk'. For the last five years you have been attracted to it, not for the rewards, but for the simple fact that nobody has ever yet emerged victorious from the labyrinth. You intend to make this the year in which a Champion is crowned! Gathering up a few belongings, you set off immediately. Two days' walk takes you west to the coast, where you enter the cursed Port Blacksand. Wasting no time in that city of thieves, you buy your passage on a small boat sailing north to where the River Kok meets the sea, and from there you take a raft up-river for four days, until finally you arrive in Fang.

The Trial begins in three days' time, and the town is in an almost hysterical mood of excitement. You register your entry with the officials and are given a violet scarf to tie around your arm, informing everyone of your status. For three days you enjoy Fang's greatest hospitality and are treated like a demigod. During the long merriment, you almost forget your purpose in Fang; but the evening before the Trial, the magnitude of the task ahead begins to dominate your thoughts. Later, you are taken to a special guest-house and shown to your room. There is a splendid four-poster bed with satin sheets to help you rest. But there is little time left for sleep.

Just before dawn a trumpet call awakens you from vivid dreams of flaming pits and giant black spiders. Minutes later, there is a knock on your door, and a man's voice rings out saying, 'Your challenge begins soon. Please be ready to leave in ten minutes.' You climb out of bed, walk over to the window and open the shutters. Already people are thronging the streets, moving quietly through the morning mist – spectators on their way to the labyrinth no doubt, hoping to find good vantage points from which to watch the competitors. You turn away and walk over to a wooden table on which your trusty sword lies. You pick it up and cut the air with a mighty sweep, wondering what beasts its sharp edge may soon have to meet. Then you open the door into the corridor. A small man with slanted eyes greets you with a low bow as you emerge from your bedroom. 'Please follow me,' he says. He turns to his left and walks quickly towards the stairs at the end of the corridor.

Leaving your guest-house, he darts down narrow alleyways between houses, and you have to walk quickly to keep up with him. Soon you come into a wide dirt road lined with cheering crowds. When they see your violet scarf, they cheer even louder and start showering you with flowers. The long shadows cast by the people in front of you shrink as the bright yellow sun rises higher in the morning sky. Standing there in front of the noisy and vibrant crowd, you feel strangely alone, aware of your coming ordeal. Suddenly you feel a tug on your shirt and see your small guide eagerly beckoning you to follow him. Ahead you see the looming hillside and the dark mouth of a tunnel disappearing into its inner depths. As you get closer, you notice two great stone pillars on either side of the tunnel entrance. The pillars are covered with ornate carvings: writhing serpents, demons, deities, each

seeming to scream a silent warning to those who would pass beyond them.

You see Baron Sukumvit himself standing by the entrance, waiting to greet the contenders in the Trial of Champions. You count five others standing proudly in line, their violet scarves displayed for all to see. There are two bare-chested Barbarians dressed in furs. They stand completely motionless, legs straight and slightly apart, arms thrust forward to rest on the hilts of their long, double-headed battleaxes. A sleek, elven woman with golden hair and feline green eyes is adjusting the cross-belt of daggers wrapped around her leather tunic. Of the two remaining men, one is covered from head to foot in iron-plate armour with a plumed helmet and a crested shield; the other is cloaked in black robes, only his dark eyes showing between the swathes of his black face-scarves. Long knives, a wire garrotte and other silent death-weapons hang from his belt. The five contenders acknowledge your arrival with almost imperceptible nods of the head, and you turn to face the exultant crowd for the last time. Suddenly a hush falls over the crowd as Baron Sukumvit steps forward holding six bamboo sticks. You draw one from his outstretched hand and read the word 'Fifth'. Then the Trial begins.

The Knight is first. He salutes the crowd before disappearing into the tunnel, and is followed half an hour later by the elf. Next goes a Barbarian and then the dark assassin. Now it is your turn to salute the crowd. Holding your violet scarf aloft, you take one final deep breath of cool fresh air before turning to pass between the stone-pillared gateway into Sukumvit's corridors of power, to face unknown perils on 'The Walk' through the mighty baron's Deathtrap Dungeon.

NOW TURN OVER

1

The clamour of the excited spectators gradually fades behind you as you venture deep into the gloom of the cavern tunnel.

Large crystals hang from the tunnel roof at twenty-metre intervals, radiating a soft light, just enough for you to see your way. As your eyes gradually become accustomed to the near darkness, you begin to see movement all around. Spiders and beetles crawling up and down the chiselled walls disappear quickly into cracks and crevices as they sense your approach; rats and mice scurry along the floor ahead of you. Droplets of water drip into small pools with an eerie plopping sound which echoes down the tunnel. The air is cold, moist and dank. After walking slowly along the tunnel for about five minutes, you arrive at a stone table standing against the wall to your left. On it there are six boxes, one of which has your name painted on its lid. If you wish to open the box, turn to **270**. If you prefer to continue walking north, turn to **66**.

2

The Scorpion manages to hold you in its pincers long enough to flick its segmented tail forward over its head and sting you with its poisonous barb. The effect is fatal and you slump to the ground in the Arena of Death, wondering whether Throm will win through.

3

The Gnome shakes his head and says, 'I am afraid you have failed the Trial of Champions. Baron Sukumvit's Deathtrap Dungeon will keep its secrets for another year, as you will not be allowed to leave here. You are appointed my servant for the rest of your days, to prepare and modify the dungeon for future contestants. Perhaps in another life you will succeed . . .'

4

In the total darkness you do not see the pipe's downward turn. You slip and, unable to get a grip on the slimy pipe, slide over the edge. Your screams echo down the pipe as you fall the fifty metres to the bottom. You have failed the Trial of Champions.

5

You crawl along the floor and find yourself in the lair of a tribe of TROGLODYTES. As you creep past them, your scabbard bangs against a rock on the floor. *Test your Luck.* If you are Lucky, turn to **185**. If you are Unlucky, turn to **395**.

6

Knowing that the Manticore will fire the spikes in its tail at you, you run for cover behind one of the pillars. Before you reach it, a volley of spikes flies through the air and one of them sinks into your arm. Lose 2 STAMINA points. If you are still alive, you waste no time and attack the Manticore with your sword before it has time to unleash more of its deadly spikes.

MANTICORE   SKILL 11   STAMINA 11

If you win, turn to **364**.

7

Before you have time to reach a doorway, the boulder is upon you. You cry out in pain and terror as it crushes you to the floor. Your adventure ends here.

8

The Mirror Demon grabs you by the wrist. Immediately it starts to pull you towards the mirror. Its strength is incredible, and, despite all your efforts, you cannot prevent it from pulling you relentlessly towards the mirror. When it touches the mirror, it seems to disappear straight through it. With horror you see your own arm disappear, followed by the rest of your body. You are now in a mirror world of another dimension, from which you can never return.

9

The Hobgoblins have nothing of any use to you on them, so you decide to open the bag on the floor. Inside you find a corked earthenware jug. You uncork it and sniff the liquid inside. It smells sharp and acrid. If you wish to drink some of the liquid, turn to **158**. If you wish to dip a piece of cloth in it, turn to **375**.

10

Still running as fast as you can, you reach into your backpack and pull out the wooden tube. You plan to lie under the surface of the water, breathing through the tube. With luck, the Troglodytes will assume that you will be swept to your death down-river as the torrent disappears into the depths of the mountain. You seize the tube between your teeth and lower yourself into the water. Holding on to one of the underwater bridge pillars, you keep perfectly still for ten minutes. When you finally think the Troglodytes have gone, you rise to the surface and look around. There is nobody to be seen, so you climb out of the river and cross the bridge to the northern bank. Any remaining Provisions you may have are now sodden and inedible. Cross them off your *Adventure Sheet*. You continue to walk through the vast cavern until at last you see a tunnel in the far wall. You walk down it until you come to a heavy wooden door, which is locked. If you have an iron key, turn to **86**. If you do not have a key, turn to **276**.

11

You look down and see the crumpled bodies of the Flying Guardians lying motionless on the floor. You start to prise out the idol's emerald eye with the tip of your sword. At last it comes free, and you are surprised by its weight. Hoping that it may be of use later, you put it in your backpack. If you now wish to prise out the right eye, turn to **140**. If you would rather climb down the idol, turn to **46**.

12

The door opens into a large, candle-lit room filled with the most extraordinarily lifelike statues of knights and warriors. A white-haired old man dressed in tattered rags suddenly jumps out from behind one of the statues and starts to giggle. Though he looks like a fool, the sparkle in his eyes makes you think there is more to him than is apparent. In a high-pitched voice he says, 'Oh good, another stone for my garden. I'm glad you have come to join your friends. Now, I'm a fair man and so I'll ask you a question. If you answer correctly, I'll let you go free – but if your answer is wrong, I'll turn you to stone!' He starts to chuckle again, obviously pleased with your arrival. Will you:

Wait for his question?	Turn to 382
Attack him with your sword?	Turn to 195
Make a run for the door?	Turn to 250

13

The tunnel makes a sudden turn to the left and heads north for as far as you can see. The footprints you are following start to peter out as the tunnel becomes gradually drier. Soon you are beyond the dripping roof and the pools on the floor. You notice the air becoming hotter and you find yourself panting even though you are walking quite slowly. In a small recess on the left-hand wall you see a section of bamboo standing on its end. Lifting it down, you see it is filled with a clear liquid. Your throat is painfully dry and you feel a little dizzy from the heat in the tunnel. If you wish to drink the liquid, turn to **147**. If you do not want to risk drinking the liquid and would rather continue north, turn to **182**.

14
The tunnel leads into a dark chamber covered in thick cobwebs. Clawing your way through them, you trip over a wooden casket. If you wish to try to open the casket, turn to **157**. If you would rather continue north, turn to **310**.

15
A tickling sensation runs down your spine as you crawl carefully out of the room. Back in the tunnel you heave a sigh of relief, throw the skull back into the room and slam the door shut. Pleased with your good fortune, you set off west once again. Turn to **74**.

16

You just have time to hear the Gnome say, 'Three skulls' before a white bolt of energy shoots out from the lock into your chest, knocking you unconscious. Roll one die, add 1 to the number and reduce your STAMINA by the total. If you are still alive, you come to and are told by the Gnome to try again. You chose the wrong gems last time, so you won't try that combination again.

A	B	C	
Emerald	Diamond	Sapphire	Turn to **16**
Diamond	Sapphire	Emerald	Turn to **392**
Sapphire	Emerald	Diamond	Turn to **177**
Emerald	Sapphire	Diamond	Turn to **287**
Diamond	Emerald	Sapphire	Turn to **132**
Sapphire	Diamond	Emerald	Turn to **249**

17

You are not strong enough to force open the heavy door. The water is now waist-high and you are exhausted from your efforts. The water level rises quickly and you find yourself floating ever upwards until your face is pressed against the ceiling. You are soon completely immersed and unable to hold your breath any longer. Your adventure ends here.

18

Luckily for you, the cobra's fangs sink into your leather wristband. The snake recoils quickly, ready to strike again, as the Dwarf tells you to have another try. Roll two dice. If the total is the same as or less than your SKILL, turn to 55. If the total is greater than your SKILL, turn to 202.

19

You cannot resist the Medusa's beguiling gaze as she looks into your eyes. You feel your limbs begin to stiffen and you panic helplessly as you turn to stone. Your adventure ends here.

20

Only your incredible strength could withstand the poisonous spider's bite. However, you are weakened and you notice your hand trembling as you pocket the Gold Piece. Reduce your SKILL by 1 point. You curse the person who dropped the backpack and set off north again. Turn to 279.

21

The wound has had no effect on the Bloodbeast, and it continues to attack you as furiously as before. Continue your combat and as soon as you win your next Attack Round, *Test your Luck*. If you are Lucky, turn to 97. If you are Unlucky, turn to 116.

22

Although you are slightly uneasy in each other's company, knowing that there can only be one winner in the Trial of Champions, you are both content to share in the benefits of a temporary alliance. You begin to tell each other of your exploits so far, of the monsters and traps encountered and the dangers overcome. Walking along, you soon come to the edge of a wide pit. It is too deep and dark to see the bottom. The Barbarian offers to lower you to the bottom with his rope, saying he has a torch which he can light for you to use. Will you:

Accept the Barbarian's offer?	Turn to **63**
Offer to lower him down if he is so eager to investigate the pit?	Turn to **184**
Suggest that you both jump over the pit instead?	Turn to **311**

23

The paper bears a simple warning written in dried blood: 'Beware the Trialmasters'. You replace the paper on its nail and run back down the tunnel to rejoin the Barbarian. Turn to **154**.

24

Set back in an arched alcove in the tunnel wall you see an ornate wooden chair carved in the shape of a demon-like bird of prey. If you wish to sit in the chair, turn to **324**. If you would rather keep going north, turn to **188**.

25

Although the temperature in the tunnel is higher than you could normally tolerate, the liquid from the bamboo pipe keeps you alive. Turn to **197**.

26

The pill makes you feel dull and lethargic. Lose two SKILL points. The Dwarf tells you that you can now progress to the second stage of the test. He reaches for a wicker basket and tells you that there is a snake inside it. He tips up the basket and the snake drops on to the floor; it is a cobra and it rears up into the air ready to strike. The Dwarf says he wants to test your reactions. You must grasp the cobra bare-handed below its head, avoiding its deadly fangs. You crouch down on the floor, tensing yourself for the moment at which to seize it. Roll two dice. If the total is the same as or less than your SKILL, turn to **55**. If the total is greater than your SKILL, turn to **202**.

27

You step up to the frightened man and cleave the chain with your sword. He drops to his knees and bows, thanking you over and over again. He tells you that four years ago he entered the Trial of Champions but failed. He fell down a pit and had to be rescued by a Trialmaster, one of Baron Sukumvit's dungeon administrators. He was offered a choice between death or servitude in Deathtrap Dungeon as the Trialmaster's minion. Choosing the latter, he worked like a slave until he could stand it no longer and tried to escape. Alas, he was unsuccessful and was captured by the Trialmaster's wandering Orc guards. To teach him a lesson, they cut off his hand and condemned him to a year's imprisonment in this cell. You ask him whether he has any information that might be of use to you. He scratches his head. 'Well, I haven't exactly done very well in here myself,' he says, 'but I do know that you need to collect gems and precious stones if you hope to get out. I don't know why, but there it is.' Without another word, the ragged prisoner dashes out of the room, turning left into the tunnel. You decide to keep heading north and turn right into the tunnel. Turn to **78**.

28

The Dwarf's chainmail coat is of finest-quality iron, obviously made by a master armourer. You strip it from his body and place it over your head. Add 1 SKILL point. There is nothing else of use to you in the chamber, so you decide to investigate the new tunnel. Turn to **213**.

29

The tunnel leads north for some distance before coming to a dead end. The mouth of a chute protrudes from the tunnel's eastern wall. It seems to be the only way out. You decide to risk it and climb into the chute. You slide gently down and come out in a room, landing on your back. Turn to **90**.

30

Taking a step forward, you leap towards the far edge of the pit. *Test your Luck*. If you are Lucky, turn to **160**. If you are Unlucky, turn to **319**.

31

The Gnome smiles and says, 'Good. Now, have you a sapphire in your possession?' If you do have a sapphire, turn to **376**. If you do not, turn to **3**.

32

You soon come to another junction in the tunnel. One branch leads east, but the wet footprints you have been following continue north and you decide to follow their trail. Turn to **37**.

33

It was a mistake to reach into the hole with your sword arm. It is covered with round sucker marks and feels as if it has been crushed. Lose 3 SKILL points. You peer into the hole and see the bleeding tentacle stump hanging limply. You carefully pull out the grappling iron and leather pouch, in which you find a tiny brass bell. You pack away your new possessions and head north. Turn to **292**.

34

You try to force the point of your sword under the emerald eye. Much to your surprise, the emerald shatters on contact, releasing a jet of poisonous gas straight into your face. The gas knocks you out and you release the rope, bounce down the idol and crash on to the stone floor. Your adventure ends here.

35

The tunnel continues west for several hundred metres, finally ending at some steps leading up to a closed trapdoor. You climb the steps slowly, hearing muffled voices above you. In the dim light you can see that the trapdoor is not locked. If you wish to knock on the trapdoor, turn to **333**. If you wish to burst through the trapdoor with your sword drawn, turn to **124**.

36

You run faster than you have ever run in your life before, but still the boulder is catching up on you. Roll two dice. If the total is the same as or less than both your SKILL and STAMINA scores, turn to **340**. If the total is greater than either your SKILL or STAMINA scores, turn to **7**.

37

The passage opens out into a wide cavern which is darker but much drier. Ahead you see the footprints gradually fade, then disappear. There is a large idol in the centre of the cavern, standing approximately six metres high. It has jewelled eyes, each as big as your fist. There are two giant stuffed bird-like creatures standing on either side of the idol. If you wish to climb the idol to take the jewels, turn to **351**. If you wish to walk through the cavern to the tunnel in the opposite wall, turn to **239**.

38

The man stands by silently while you gulp the water and wolf down the bread. A sharp pain grips your stomach and you fall to your knees. The old man looks at you scornfully and says, 'Well, if you will eat poisoned food, what do you expect?' Lose 3 STAMINA points. He shuffles off, leaving you writhing in pain on the floor. If you are still alive, you eventually regain enough of your strength to continue west. Turn to **109**.

39

You manage to evade the outstretched legs of the diving Giant Fly. Stepping back, you draw your sword and prepare to fight the hideous insect as it turns to attack you again.

GIANT FLY   SKILL 7   STAMINA 8

If you win, turn to **111**. You may *Escape* by running back into the tunnel to head north. Turn to **267**.

40

You call out to the Dwarf that you are ready to fight the MINOTAUR. The wooden door rises slowly and you see the fearsome beast, half man, half bull, step into the arena. Steam blows from its nostrils as it works itself up into a rage, ready to attack. Suddenly it rushes forward, swinging its double-headed axe.

MINOTAUR   SKILL 9   STAMINA 9

If you win, turn to 163.

41

You walk slowly over to the alcove, carefully checking the floor for any more hidden traps. You see that the goblet contains a sparkling red liquid. Will you:

Drink the red liquid?	Turn to 98
Leave the goblet and walk back to search the Barbarian (if you have not done so already)?	Turn to 126
Leave the chamber to continue west?	Turn to 83

42

The cobra's fangs sink deep into your wrist and you feel its poison starting to creep through your body. Lose 5 STAMINA points. If you are still alive, the Dwarf has no mercy but tells you to try again. Roll two dice. If the total is the same as or less than your SKILL, turn to 55. If the total is greater than your SKILL, turn to 202.

43

The tunnel turns sharply to the right and continues north for as far as you can see. There is a door in the left-hand wall which is ajar. You hear someone cry for help from the other side of the door. If you wish to open it, turn to **200**. If you would rather continue north, turn to **316**.

44

You are only a few metres from the doorway when you hear the old man behind you utter some strange words. Instantly your muscles harden and you feel your skin becoming taut. You start to panic, but there is nothing you can do to stop the petrifaction of your body. Your adventure ends here.

45

The razor-sharp disc thuds into your back with terrible effect. Lose 1 SKILL point and 4 STAMINA points. If you are still alive, you struggle to pull the disc from your back as the Ninja throws yet another one at you. Turn to **312**.

46

You lower yourself carefully down the idol and, wasting no more time in the cavern, run forward to the tunnel in the northern wall. Turn to **239**.

47

Have you got a hollow wooden tube? If you have, turn to **10**. If you have not, turn to **335**.

48

Only your immense strength and grim determination keep you from falling unconscious to the floor. You grit your teeth and press on resolutely. Turn to **197**.

49

You peep round the corner and see two small creatures running away from you. Both are dressed in baggy clothes and wear pointed floppy hats. They are mischievous LEPRECHAUNS. If you wish to follow them, turn to **205**. If you would rather walk back to the last junction to head north, turn to **241**.

50

You wake to find Throm pulling the ring off your finger. He puts it on the floor and crushes it with the head of his battleaxe. Then, grunting to show his disapproval of you, he strides off east. You stand up slowly and stagger off after him. Turn to **221**.

51

The Hobgoblins are unprepared for your attack, and you are able to kill the first one before he can draw his sword. You turn to face the remaining Hobgoblin, who snarls at you with hatred.

HOBGOBLIN   SKILL 6   STAMINA 5

If you win, turn to **9**.

52

As you open the book, it begins to disintegrate and the pages turn to dust in your hands. You manage to keep a few fragments and read the handwritten script. The book appears to be about monsters, and from what you can make out it contains a full description of a monster called the Bloodbeast. It is a horrific bloated creature with tough, spiny skin and facial blisters which burst open to become mock eyes, evolved to hide the Bloodbeast's only weak spot – its real eyes. Bloodbeasts usually dwell in pools of fetid slime which give off a poisonous gas. This gas is so strong that it can easily knock people unconscious. The Bloodbeast, although too bulbous to haul itself out of its slime pool, has a long and vicious tongue which it wraps around its victims before it drags them into its pool. As the victim's flesh starts to decompose in the vile slime, the Bloodbeast will feed from it. You tell Throm about the grotesque Bloodbeast, but he merely shrugs his shoulders and tells you to get going. If you have not done so already, you may open the black book – turn to **138**. Otherwise you must continue north with Throm – turn to **369**.

53

The Bloodbeast is too bulbous to climb out of its pool, but its long tongue whips out and tries to wrap itself around your leg. Fortunately, you have fallen beyond its reach. The air at ground level does not contain any of the poisonous fumes, but you wake with a pain in your throat. You cover your mouth with your sleeve so that you can breathe through it, and decide what to do. If you wish to run round the pool towards the tunnel, turn to **370**. If you wish to attack the Bloodbeast with your sword, turn to **348**.

54

The lasso loosens itself and you are able to shake it free of the idol's neck. It falls to the floor with a loud clatter. You quickly coil the rope up again and put it in your backpack. Wasting no more time in the cavern, you run forward to the tunnel in the northern wall. Turn to **239**.

55

55

With lightning speed, you thrust your hand out and grip the cobra just below its open mouth. You lift it up and, arm outstretched, dangle it in front of the Dwarf. He doesn't flinch but says in his calm expressionless way, 'Please put the cobra back in the basket and prepare for the final part of the test. Follow me.' You do what he says and follow him back into the chamber, where Throm is pacing up and down, obviously ill at ease. You wave to him while the Dwarf opens a second secret door and tells you to walk on through and wait for him. Again you comply, and you find yourself in another circular room, although this one resembles a small arena. The floor is covered with sand, and a small balcony runs around the arena wall. Opposite the secret door by which you entered is an ominous-looking wooden door. Suddenly you hear a shout, and you look up to see the smiling Dwarf standing on the balcony. He throws two pieces of paper down to you. On one of them, the words NO CROP IS are written; on the other, RUIN MOAT. In his ever-calm voice he says, 'If you rearrange the letters of the words, you will find the names of two creatures. You may choose which one to fight in my Arena of Death.' If you can identify the creature by rearranging the letters NO CROP IS, turn to **143**. If you can identify the creature by rearranging the letters RUIN MOAT, turn to **40**. If you cannot identify either of the creatures, turn to **347**.

56

You see that the obstruction is a large, brown, boulder-like object. You touch it with your hand and are surprised to find that it is soft and spongy. If you wish to try to climb over it, turn to **373**. If you wish to slice it open with your sword, turn to **215**.

57

Although you check the chest carefully for any hidden devices, you are unable to see the trap inside it. As you lift the lid, an iron ball hanging on a cord swings back, shattering the glass capsule fixed inside the lid. A cloud of poisonous gas is instantly released into the air and you stagger back coughing and spluttering. Lose 4 STAMINA points. If you are still alive, turn to **198**.

58

You step slowly between the poles, taking care not to touch any of them. Roll two dice. If the total is the same as or less than your SKILL score, turn to **80**. If the total is greater than your SKILL score, turn to **246**.

59

Ahead in the far distance you hear the sound of slow footsteps coming towards you. Unsure of who or what might be approaching, you look around for a place to hide. You find a large crack in the tunnel wall which lies in shadow. If you wish to stand your ground with your sword drawn, turn to **341**. If you would rather hide in the shadows, turn to **283**.

The tunnel ends at a large oak door. Throm wastes no time in testing the handle and is somewhat surprised to find the door unlocked. He pushes it open and walks into a torch-lit chamber. Sitting alone on an ornate chair is a DWARF, who bids you enter the chamber. As you do so, the oak door swings shut behind you. 'Adventurers, you have done well to get this far,' says the Dwarf in a deep voice. 'However, as you both know, there can only be one winner in the Trial of Champions. As Trial-master, it is my duty to Baron Sukumvit to let only the most able continue. Therefore, I must devise a test of wits and strength to eliminate one of you. Please do not attempt to dispose of me. It would be utterly pointless, for, as you can see, there is no obvious way out of this chamber and only I know where the hidden exit lies. Now if you would care to decide between you who will go first, I shall make the necessary preparations.' You look at Throm, suddenly angry that your effective partnership might come to an end. He leans over and whispers in your ear that you should try to kill the Dwarf and worry about the exit later. If you wish to join Throm in attacking the Dwarf, turn to **179**. If you would rather persuade Throm to go through with the Dwarf's test, turn to **365**.

61

Despite the terrible ringing sound in your ears, you hear footsteps coming down the tunnel. Your loud screams have attracted a tunnel guardian. Standing over you is a HOBGOBLIN. His face bears a sickly smile as he presses the point of his sword against your neck. You are unable to defend yourself and prevent the Hobgoblin from running you through. Your adventure ends here.

62

The Gnome jumps in the air, yelling, 'Well done – nobody has ever managed to find all three gems before! Now get ready for the final test, which I will explain once and once only. As you can see, the lock on this door has three slots, labelled A, B and C, each of which is built to accept a specific gem. You have to put one of your three gems in each of the slots in the correct order. If you manage this at the first attempt, fine. However, if you put the gems in the wrong slots, you will be blasted by a bolt of energy from the lock, causing you injury. Anyway, as I said, I am allowed to help you a little. If you place one gem in its correct slot but get the other two wrong, I shall shout, "One crown and two skulls." If you place all three gems incorrectly, I shall shout, "Three skulls." You will be allowed to try again and again until you either succeed or die. Are you ready?' You signal your readiness with a nod of the head, and walk forward to place the three gems in the slots. Decide which gems you will place in the labelled slots on the next page:

A	B	C	
Emerald	Diamond	Sapphire	Turn to **16**
Diamond	Sapphire	Emerald	Turn to **392**
Sapphire	Emerald	Diamond	Turn to **177**
Emerald	Sapphire	Diamond	Turn to **287**
Diamond	Emerald	Sapphire	Turn to **132**
Sapphire	Diamond	Emerald	Turn to **249**

63

You tie the rope around your waist and take hold of the lighted torch given to you by Throm, as your Barbarian ally calls himself. Taking hold of the slack rope, Throm lowers you slowly over the edge of the pit and down into the dark depths below. You can see by the light of the torch that the sides of the pit are extremely smooth. You drop about twenty metres before hitting the bottom of the pit. There you see another tunnel heading north and you call up to Throm and tell him of your discovery. He calls back, saying that he is going to tie the rope around a protruding rock on the edge of the pit and will come down and join you. You hear him climbing down and soon you are together again. Throm retrieves his rope by shaking it off the rock, and you set off north along the new tunnel. Turn to **194**.

64

As soon as you put the ring on your finger, your whole body starts to shake. Roll two dice. If the total is the same as or less than your SKILL score, turn to **115**. If the total is greater than your SKILL score, turn to **190**.

65

Have you drunk a Potion found inside a black leather book? If you have, turn to **345**. If you have not drunk it, turn to **372**.

66

After walking down the tunnel for a few minutes, you come to a junction. A white arrow painted on one wall points west. On the floor you can see wet footprints made by those who entered before you. It is hard to be sure, but it looks as though three of them followed the direction of the arrow, while one decided to go east. If you wish to head west, turn to **293**. If you wish to head east, turn to **119**.

67

You grab one of the underwater bridge pillars and cling to it, holding your breath. Meanwhile the Troglodytes reach the river bank and decide that you must have been swept to your death down-river as it disappears into the depths of the mountain. By now your lungs are bursting for air. *Test your Luck* again. If you are Lucky, turn to **146**. If you are Unlucky, turn to **219**.

68

You walk down the passage and soon find yourself standing at the edge of a deep, dark pit. The passage continues east on the other side of the pit. You think you could probably jump over the pit, but you are not sure. There is a rope hanging down from the ceiling over the centre of the pit. Will you:

Throw your shield over the pit and jump after it?	Turn to **271**
Jump over the pit carrying all your possessions?	Turn to **30**
Reach for the rope with your sword to enable you to swing across the pit?	Turn to **212**

69

Ivy does not notice you opening the door. You slip out of her room, close the door quietly behind you and find yourself at the end of another tunnel. Turn to 305.

70

You just manage to dive to the side before the boulder smashes into the tunnel floor, splitting the stone. As you dust yourself off, you suddenly notice daylight at the end of the tunnel. You run forward towards a beautiful sight of blue sky and green trees. Running out of the tunnel, you expect to be greeted by cheering crowds, but are horrified at what you do see. There is no hero's welcome from the people all around you. All are dead. You are in fact standing in a cold chamber littered with armoured skeletons and bodies – the exit to victory was just an illusion! Only the corpses of past adventurers are real. You run back towards the tunnel, but hit an invisible barrier. You are trapped and destined to end your days in the chamber of the dead.

71

Once again you reach for the parchment, only this time it is lying amidst a pile of broken bones. Unfolding it, you see a map of a room with a drawing of a hideous creature inside it. Beneath the monster is a rhyme which reads:

> 'Should you meet the Manticore,
> Of its tail beware.
> Shield yourself against the spikes
> Flying through the air.'

You fold up the piece of parchment and put it in your backpack. Repeating the rhyme over and over to yourself, you walk across to the alcove. Turn to **128**.

72

The Mirror shatters, sending fragments of glass flying everywhere. The Mirror Demon's four faces cry out in agony, and cracks appear all over them. Then they too shatter and fall to the floor in a pile of broken glass. Unfortunately, you cut your sword arm badly while smashing the mirror. Although your strength is unaffected, your weaponskill is diminished. Lose 2 SKILL points before continuing your journey north. Turn to **122**.

73

If you have not done so already, you may walk back to search the Barbarian – turn to **126**. Otherwise, leave the chamber to continue west – turn to **83**.

74

The tunnel takes a sharp right turn and you find yourself in a sort of gallery lined with mirrors for some twenty metres. A human skeleton appears to be pulled halfway through the mirror along the right-hand wall. Suddenly a grotesque being with four arms and four screaming faces emerges from the mirror, barring your way ahead. It walks slowly towards you, each arm outstretched to grab you. It is a MIRROR DEMON from another dimensional plane, come to take your spirit. Will you:

Make a wish (if you are wearing a Ring of Wishes?)	Turn to **265**
Try to smash the mirrors?	Turn to **300**
Attack the Mirror Demon with your sword?	Turn to **327**

75

You rub the liquid into your wounds, but they do not heal. Staring into the empty bottle, you wonder what exactly the liquid was. If you have not done so already, you may open the red book – turn to **52**. Otherwise, you must continue north with Throm – turn to **369**.

76

You step round the great bulk of the dead Rock Grub and peer into the darkness of its borehole. You can only see a few metres, but are able to make out that it inclines slightly and is wet from the secreted slime of the Rock Grub. If you wish to explore the borehole, turn to **317**. If you would rather walk west along the tunnel, turn to **117**.

77

You stagger through the open doorway into another tunnel, at the end of which is the welcome sight of daylight. Much to your surprise, you see the Gnome lying dead halfway down the tunnel. A crossbow bolt protrudes from the side of his head. The Gnome, in his bid for freedom, has fallen foul of Baron Sukumvit's final trap. You walk past him and out into brilliant sunshine. Turn to **400**.

78

There is an open pipe in the right-hand wall, about a metre in diameter. It is too dark to see far down it. You shout into it and hear your voice echoing down the iron pipe until eventually the sound fades away. If you wish to crawl down the pipe, turn to **301**. If you would rather continue north, turn to **142**.

79

You grip the arms of the chair tightly, half expecting a surge of energy or pain to rush through your body. *Test your Luck.* If you are Lucky, turn to **106**. If you are Unlucky, turn to **383**.

80

You take your time and manage to step over the last pole without having touched any of them. You hurry on east, still following the two pairs of footprints. Turn to **313**.

81

The only furniture in the Goblin's room is a table, two chairs and a cupboard on the wall. There are two closed doors, one in the west wall and the other in the north wall. Will you:

Open the cupboard?	Turn to **307**
Open the west door?	Turn to **263**
Open the north door?	Turn to **136**

82

As the Pit Fiend slams its body against the wall, you let go of the rope and drop safely to the floor. You run towards the double doors and are relieved to feel them swing open as you push on them. You let them swing shut behind you and head north along the tunnel. Turn to **214**.

83

The passage soon leads to a junction. You notice more footprints on the floor, possibly as many as three pairs, heading north from the south passage. You decide to follow them. Turn to **37**.

84

Roll two dice. If the total is more than eight, turn to **152**. If the total is eight or less, turn to **121**.

85

Before you are able to do anything else, the old man mumbles a few strange words into the air. You feel your muscles harden and your skin go taut. You start to panic, but there is nothing you can do to stop the petrifaction of your body. Your adventure ends here.

86

The key turns in the lock and the door opens into a four-way intersection of the tunnel. There is nothing to be seen either to east or to west apart from the now familiar ceiling crystals giving off their dim light. Suddenly you hear a voice calling you, 'This way, this way. You are on the right track.' It seems to be coming from somewhere directly ahead of you. Your curiosity gets the better of you and you decide to walk towards the beckoning voice. Turn to **187**.

87

The door opens into a large room. Turn to **381**.

88

As soon as they see you, the TROGLODYTES raise their bows and run to surround you. To your horror, their leader then steps forward and declares that you are their prisoner and must subject yourself to trial by their ancient rite, the Run of the Arrow. If you are willing to take part in the Run of the Arrow, turn to **343**. If you would rather try to fight your way out, turn to **268**.

89

Back on solid ground once again on the cavern floor, you try to shake the rope off the idol's neck. *Test your Luck.* If you are Lucky, turn to **54**. If you are Unlucky, turn to **261**.

90

As soon as you stand up, you are confronted by the most repulsive sight you have ever laid eyes on. There in front of you, wallowing in a circular pool of fetid slime, is a bulbous creature too horrible to be believed. Its body is green and covered all over with fearsome-looking spikes. Its face is a mass of crimson blisters, one of which suddenly bursts to reveal yet another of its many sinister, all-seeing eyes. A narrow path runs around the edge of the pool and leads into another tunnel in the far wall. If you have previously read details about the loathsome BLOODBEAST in a leather-bound book, turn to **172**. If you have not read this book, turn to **357**.

91

The Orc's morning star thuds into your arm, knocking your sword to the floor. You must fight them bare-handed, reducing your SKILL by 4 for the duration of the combat. Fortunately, the tunnel is too narrow for both Orcs to attack you at once. Fight them one at a time.

	SKILL	STAMINA
First ORC	5	5
Second ORC	6	4

If you win, turn to 257.

92

Summoning all your strength, you deal the Mirror Demon one final blow with your sword. With an ear-splitting sound, cracks begin to run across its faces and limbs. Its many mouths cry out in the agony of its death throes before the Demon shatters completely and falls to the ground in a pile of tiny fragments. You heave a huge sigh of relief and then hurry on past. Turn to 122.

93

The door opens into a small dark room, which is empty apart from a sturdy wooden chest lying on a shelf on the far wall. The floor is thick with dust, and you can clearly see fresh footprints leading from the door to the chest and back again. You wonder whether one of your rivals is still ahead of you on 'The Walk', or whether the chest has only recently been placed on the shelf by one of the Trialmasters. If you wish to enter the room and open the chest, turn to **284**. If you would rather keep walking down the tunnel, turn to **230**.

94

Taking a deep breath, you lean over the pit and plunge your forearm into the mass of wriggling worms. They are cold and clammy and feel extremely nasty, but at least they are harmless and you are able to seize the dagger by the hilt. You give it a hard tug and it comes away from the crack in which the tip was embedded. Admiring its beauty, and wondering whether it might once have belonged to some luckless contestant, you put the opal-studded dagger firmly in your belt and leave the cavern. Turn to **174**.

95

The iron ring is attached to a small trapdoor. It lifts up easily, and inside a small compartment you find a finely crafted shield made of the purest iron. Marvelling at its splendour, you strap it on to your arm. Add 1 SKILL point. You walk towards the double doors and push them open. Turn to **248**.

96

Your second blow also fails to smash the mirror. The Mirror Demon reaches out, grabs your wrist and starts pulling you towards the mirror. Its strength is incredible, and, despite all your efforts, you cannot resist. With every second you come closer to the mirror. When the Mirror Demon touches the mirror, it seems to disappear straight through it. With horror you see your own arm disappear through the mirror too, and the rest of your body soon follows. You are now in a mirror world of another dimension, from which you can never return.

97

Unknown to you, the Bloodbeast has only one weakness: its real eyes. More by chance than by design, you plunge your blade deep into one of them, and the Bloodbeast immediately slumps back into its pool. After a few massive convulsions, it sinks beneath the oily surface of the pool. Not waiting to see whether it will recover, you run into the tunnel, anxious to get away from the Bloodbeast's toxic chamber as fast as possible. Turn to **134**.

98

Lifting the goblet releases a sprung catch, and a dart shoots out of the wooden table leg. *Test your Luck.* If you are Lucky, turn to **105**. If you are Unlucky, turn to **235**.

99

Smiling, you tell Ivy that you think she and Sourbelly look very alike. Then, while she stares admiringly at the painting, you pick up a broken stool, creep up behind her and smash her over the back of the head with it as hard as you can. To your immense relief, she slumps unconscious to the floor. If you wish to search her room, turn to **266**. If not, leave by the door in the east wall. You find yourself standing at the end of a tunnel. Turn to **305**.

100

Only a few metres further down the passage, you see another closed door in the left-hand wall. The letter X is scratched into its centre panel. Putting your ear to the door, you listen intently but can hear nothing. If you wish to open the door, turn to **87**. If you would rather keep walking north, turn to **217**.

101

The river current is quite strong and, encumbered by your armour and backpack, you are unable to swim against it. Within seconds you are swept under the bridge. Standing on the river bank, the Troglodytes look on laughing and jeering as you drift to your death down-river in the depths of the mountain.

102

You enter a room which is small and completely empty. As soon as you are inside, the door slams shut behind you. Suddenly a voice booms out of nowhere, shouting, 'Welcome to Deathtrap Dungeon, the ingenious killer labyrinth of my master. Adventurer, I trust you will pay your respects to my master by shouting out his name?' Will you shout:

Hail, Sukumvit?	Turn to **133**
Sukumvit is a worm?	Turn to **251**

103

You breathe in the poisonous gas and start to choke. Lose 3 STAMINA points. If you are still alive, turn to 77.

104

Reacting quickly, you manage to jump over the outstretched tongue and run into the tunnel, leaving the Bloodbeast wallowing in its pool to await another victim. Turn to **134**.

105

Your reflexes are sharp and you quickly jump aside. The dart whistles past, only just missing you, and thuds into the opposite wall. You see the goblet lying on the floor and the red liquid running away in rivulets over the grey stone. At least the goblet may be of use, so you put it in your backpack. If you have not done so already, you may walk back to search the Barbarian – turn to **126**. Otherwise, leave the chamber to continue west – turn to **83**.

106

Squeezing the arm of the chair triggers a secret panel which springs into the air. You find a glass phial lying in a cavity. You pick it up and read the label: 'Doppelganger Potion – one dose only. This liquid will make your body take on the shape of any nearby being.' You place the strange potion in your backpack and continue north. Turn to **188**.

107

You come to an arched doorway set in the right-hand wall of the tunnel. The heavy stone door is closed, but there is an iron latch and a round handle. If you wish to try the door, turn to **168**. If instead you wish to continue along the tunnel, turn to **267**.

108

There is a large panel of glass in the left-hand wall of the tunnel. Through it you can see a bright, torch-lit room teeming with GIANT INSECTS of every possible description. Bees, wasps, beetles, ticks – even the mites are over six centimetres long. The noise is threatening. In the middle of the room, a jewelled crown lies on top of a small table. What looks like a large diamond is set in the middle of the crown. Will you:

Break the glass and try to snatch the crown?	Turn to **394**
Continue west?	Turn to **59**
Return to the junction to head north?	Turn to **14**

109

You arrive at another junction in the tunnel. If you wish to keep heading west, turn to **43**. If you wish to go north, turn to **24**.

110

The tunnel soon takes another sharp right turn. Following it east, you arrive at a strange obstruction: a line of twelve wooden poles across the tunnel. They are fixed to the walls about half a metre off the floor and spaced a metre apart. If you wish to step between the poles, turn to **58**. If you wish to walk across the top of the poles, turn to **223**.

111

You wipe the vile yellow slime from the blade of your sword and walk quickly to the door, back into the tunnel and head north. Turn to **267**.

112

Apart from two portions of your Provisions which were saturated and are now inedible, all your other possessions remain intact. You repack them carefully inside your backpack and set off north again. Turn to **356**.

113

The wooden ball whistles past the skull, hitting the far wall with a loud 'crack'. If you wish to try again with the other ball, turn to **371**. If you have already thrown twice, or do not wish to throw again, you may decide to close the door and continue west along the tunnel – turn to **74**.

114

The Caveman is wearing a leather wristband with four small rats' skulls hanging from it. If you wish to put it on your own wrist, turn to **336**. If you would rather set off north again, turn to **298**.

115

Your body continues to vibrate intensely and you feel as if you are about to pass out. But your strength is great, and you manage to withstand the tremendous shock to your system. Finally you calm down and begin to feel the ring's beneficial powers working on you. Add 3 STAMINA points. You see Throm looking at you anxiously, so you reassure him that you are fully recovered. He strides off east and you follow him eagerly. Turn to **221**.

116

You cannot believe that the Bloodbeast is unaffected by its new wound. You hesitate a moment too long and it lunges forward, cracking your skull with its jaws. Then it drags you into its pool, where you will be predigested and later consumed by the hideous creature.

117

After a long walk down the tunnel, you come to a dead end. A large mirror reaching from the ceiling to the floor hangs on the end wall, and in the dim light you can just about make out your own reflection. If you wish to take a closer look in the mirror, turn to **329**. If you would rather make the long walk back to the last junction in the tunnel in order to head east, turn to **135**.

118

Despite the stalactites crashing all around, you manage to dash through the archway without injury. You look round and see Throm thundering towards you, one arm held over his head for protection. He dashes into the tunnel and leans against the cold wall, panting heavily. He apologizes for starting the rock-fall and offers you his hand to shake. You tell Throm that maybe he should use sign language in future, even for laughing! You both smile and head east once more. Turn to **60**.

119

Ahead you can see a large obstruction on the tunnel floor, although it is too dark to make out exactly what it is. The wet footprints you have been following carry on towards the obstruction. If you want to continue east, turn to **56**. If you would rather go back to the junction and head west, turn to **293**.

120

Lying in a hole about a metre deep, you see a grappling iron and a leather pouch. If you wish to reach down for them, turn to **228**. If you would rather ignore them and continue north, turn to **292**.

121

The Dwarf looks at the dice. 'Not very good at playing the odds, are you?' he sneers. 'I regret you must suffer a penalty before you can continue.' From out of his pocket he produces two pills. One is stamped with the letter S and the other stamped with the letter L. He asks you to choose one and swallow it. If you wish to swallow the pill stamped with the letter S, turn to **26**. If you wish to swallow the other pill, turn to **354**.

122

In front of you are two flights of stone steps sep-arated by a banister of rat skulls. You may climb either the left-hand flight of steps – turn to **176** – or the right-hand flight – turn to **384**.

123

The necklace is an amulet of strength. Add 1 SKILL point and 1 STAMINA point and continue your quest north. Turn to **282**.

124

You throw the trapdoor open and run up the steps into a bright, lantern-lit room. Two GOBLINS are sharpening their short swords on a stone set in the middle of the floor. You catch them momentarily off guard, but they quickly recover and both rush forward to attack you.

	SKILL	STAMINA
First GOBLIN	5	4
Second GOBLIN	5	5

Both Goblins will have a separate attack on you in each Attack Round, but you must choose which of the two you will fight. Attack your chosen Goblin as in a normal battle. Against the other you must throw for your Attack Strength in the normal way, but even if your Attack Strength is greater you will not wound it. You must just count this as though you have defended yourself against its blow. However, if its Attack Strength is greater, it will have wounded you in the normal way. If you win, turn to **81**.

125

You tiptoe towards the door while Ivy prattles on. *Test your Luck*. If you are Lucky, turn to **69**. If you are Unlucky, turn to **139**.

126

The pouch on the Barbarian's belt is empty apart from some strange-looking dried meat wrapped in a cloth. Will you:

Eat the dried meat?	Turn to **226**
Leave the meat and walk over to the alcove (if you have not done so already)?	Turn to **41**
Leave the chamber and head west?	Turn to **83**

127

The only possible way out of the hall as far as you can see is by using the chute in the northern wall. You decide to give it a go and climb into the chute. You slide gently down and emerge into another room, landing on your back. Turn to **90**.

128

At the back of the alcove are some steps leading down into a cellar. Cobwebs brush your face as you descend. The cellar ceiling is quite low, and the floor is strewn with rubbish and debris. In the middle of the wall opposite you is an archway which leads into another crystal-lit tunnel. There are large mushrooms growing on the rubbish to your right. If you wish to step through the archway, turn to **35**. If you wish to stop to eat some of the mushrooms, turn to **233**.

129

You tie the rope to the grappling iron and hurl it over the top of the wall. Its hooks dig into the stone and you begin to haul yourself up. Peering over the top of the wall, you see an enormous dinosaur-like monster thrashing about in a sand-covered pit. Its tough hide is a mottled green colour, and it stands some ten metres tall on its muscular hind legs. Rows of razor-sharp teeth line its gigantic jaws, which open and close with bone-snapping power. There is a large double door in the wall on the far side of the pit, which appears to be the only way out of this section of the dungeon. Will you:

Lower yourself down on the rope into the pit to fight the PIT FIEND?   Turn to **349**

Throw your bone monkey charm into the pit (if you have one)?   Turn to **361**

Try to hook the PIT FIEND with the grappling iron while sitting on top of the wall?   Turn to **167**

130

The Hobgoblins stop their fight immediately. They do not understand what you are saying and snarl at you viciously. Then they draw their short swords and run forward to attack you. Fight them one at a time.

	SKILL	STAMINA
First HOBGOBLIN	7	5
Second HOBGOBLIN	6	5

If you win, turn to **9**.

131

The crossbow bolts fly over your head and thud into the opposite wall; fortunately, you are still crouching on the floor. Now that the trap has been sprung, you can leave the room by the door through which you entered. Back in the tunnel you head on west. Turn to **74**.

132

You just have time to hear the Gnome say, 'One crown and two skulls', before a white bolt of energy shoots out from the lock into your chest and knocks you unconscious. Roll one die, add 1 to the number and reduce your STAMINA by the total. If you are still alive, you come to and are told by the Gnome to try again. You know you placed one gem in the correct slot, but which one? You sigh and tentatively try a new combination.

A	B	C	
Emerald	Diamond	Sapphire	Turn to **16**
Diamond	Sapphire	Emerald	Turn to **392**
Sapphire	Emerald	Diamond	Turn to **177**
Emerald	Sapphire	Diamond	Turn to **287**
Diamond	Emerald	Sapphire	Turn to **132**
Sapphire	Diamond	Emerald	Turn to **249**

133

Once again, the mysterious voice calls out, only this time its tone is full of contempt and derision. 'So, we have a snivelling weed in our midst, do we?' sneers the voice. 'My master has a special gift for you, loathsome creep.' Suddenly water starts pouring into the room through a hole in the ceiling. It soon rises above your ankles, and there is no apparent way of escape. You wade back to the door. It is firmly locked, but in desperation you try ramming it with your shoulder. Roll two dice. If the total is the same as or less than your SKILL score, turn to **178**. If the total is greater than your SKILL score, turn to **17**.

134

The tunnel leads into a large room, its ceiling supported by several marble pillars. As you enter the room, you suddenly see a strange beast to your right. It has the body of a lion with dragon-like wings attached to it, but its head is like that of an old bearded man. If you have read the poem written on the Skeleton Warrior's parchment, turn to **222**. If you have not read this poem, turn to **247**.

135

Passing the Rock Grub's borehole on your left, you soon arrive at the junction. You take a quick look down the tunnel leading south, but do not see anybody approaching. Quickening your step, you hurry on east. Turn to **68**.

136

The door opens into another tunnel, which rises gently into the distance. After walking uphill for a while, the tunnel levels out and you soon arrive at a door in the right-hand wall, to which a withered hand is nailed. If you wish to open the door, turn to **210**. If you would rather continue north, turn to **78**.

137

Walking along the tunnel, you are surprised to see a large iron bell hanging down from the ceiling. If you wish to ring the bell, turn to **220**. If you would rather walk round it and continue west, turn to **362**.

138

The book's pages are sealed together, but a small hole has been cut out in the middle of them, just large enough to hold a small corked bottle containing a clear liquid. You show it to Throm, who holds up his hand, indicating that he does not want you to come anywhere near him with it; his distrust of things unknown is strongly evident. Will you:

Drink the liquid?	Turn to **397**
Rub the liquid into your wounds?	Turn to **75**
Open the red book (if you have not done so already)?	Turn to **52**
Leave the bottle and book to continue north with Throm?	Turn to **369**

139

As you try to escape, Ivy whirls round and picks up a broken stool. She is angry and attacks you ferociously. Lose 2 STAMINA points. If you are still alive, you manage to draw your sword and fight back.

IVY   SKILL 9   STAMINA 9

If you win, turn to **201**.

140

You try to force the point of your sword under the emerald eye. Much to your surprise, it shatters on contact, releasing a jet of poisonous gas straight into your face. The gas knocks you out and you fall backwards, bouncing down the idol to land on the stone floor. Your adventure ends here.

141

The Mirror Demon is almost on top of you when, summoning all your strength, you strike one final blow against the mirror with your sword. Roll two dice. If the total is the same as or less than your SKILL, turn to **72**. If the total is greater than your SKILL, turn to **96**.

142

There is a new branch in the tunnel on your left, and ahead you see two bodies lying on the floor. You stop and peer down the new tunnel, but seeing no doors or creatures you decide against walking down it. With your sword drawn, you walk over to where the bodies lie. Turn to **338**.

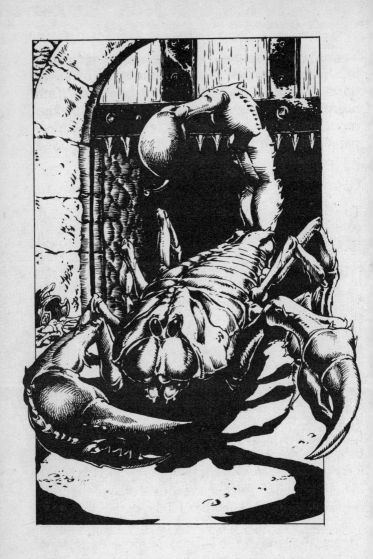

143

You call out to the Dwarf, telling him to send in the SCORPION because you are ready to fight. Slowly the wooden door rises, and a huge, grotesque black Scorpion squeezes underneath it and enters the room. You draw your sword in readiness and prepare to fight the sinister creature with its huge pincers and deadly sting.

GIANT SCORPION   SKILL 10   STAMINA 10

The Scorpion attacks you with both pincers, and you must treat each pincer as a separate creature as though you were fighting two creatures. Both pincers have a SKILL of 10 and will attack you separately in each Attack Round, but you must choose which of the two you will fight. Attack one pincer as in a normal battle. Against the other pincer you must throw for your Attack Strength in the normal way, but you will not wound it even if your Attack Strength is greater; you must count this as though you have just fended off its blow. Of course, if its Attack Strength is greater, it will have wounded you in the normal way. If, during any of the Attack Rounds, the Scorpion's Attack Strength totals 22, turn to **2**. If you manage to kill the Scorpion without it scoring an Attack Strength of 22, turn to **163**.

144

Still smiling, the old man looks at you and says quietly, 'Wrong.' Turn to **85**.

145

The Dwarf is expecting your move. Furthermore, you are not as fast as you should be because of your recent ordeal, so he easily evades your punch, saying, 'I could kill you now if I wished, but I yearn for a hand-to-hand fight.' Then he throws down his crossbow and draws an axe from his belt. Despite your fatigue, you think only of vengeance.

DWARF   SKILL 8   STAMINA 6

During each Attack Round you must reduce your Attack Strength by 2 because of your condition. If you win, turn to **28**.

146

The pain in your lungs forces you to rise to the surface for air. Fortunately, none of the Troglodytes see you and they all disperse. You climb out of the river and cross the bridge to the northern bank. Any remaining Provisions you may have are now inedible. You continue to walk through the vast cavern until at last you see a tunnel in the far wall. You walk down it until you come to a heavy wooden door which is locked. If you have an iron key, turn to **86**. If you do not have a key, turn to **276**.

147

The water in the bamboo pipe is welcomingly refreshing. Add 1 STAMINA point. It also contains a magical solution which will enable you to be exposed to melting-point temperatures without harm. Discarding the bamboo, you start off north again in good spirits. Turn to **182**.

148

There is nowhere to go except down the steps towards the barking dogs. You reach the bottom and, with your sword drawn, face the two huge black GUARD DOGS, which leap at you one at a time.

	SKILL	STAMINA
First GUARD DOG	7	7
Second GUARD DOG	7	8

If you win, turn to **175**. You may *Escape* after killing the first Guard Dog by running east down the tunnel. Turn to **315**.

149

You let go of the rope and hear it fall to the bottom of the pit. The Barbarian curses, promising to kill you if your paths should cross again. You step back and take a running jump. You land safely on the far side of the pit and continue west. Further down the tunnel, you step on a floor stone which tilts forward, triggering a trap which releases a boulder loosely set in the ceiling. You look up just as it is about to crash on top of you. *Test your Luck*. If you are Lucky, turn to **70**. If you are Unlucky, turn to **353**.

150

Having had the sense not to put your sword arm into the hole, the effects of the tentacled arm are not too serious. Lose 1 SKILL point. You reach back into the hole and pull out the grappling iron and the leather pouch. Inside the pouch you find a tiny brass bell. You pack away your new possessions and continue north. Turn to **292**.

151

As you touch the idol's emerald eye you hear a creaking sound below you. Looking down, you are shocked to see the two stuffed birds flying off. Their wings flap in jerky movements, but they are soon above you and look set to attack. Fight the FLYING GUARDIANS one at a time, but reduce your SKILL by 2 during this combat because of your restricted position.

	SKILL	STAMINA
First FLYING GUARDIAN	7	8
Second FLYING GUARDIAN	8	8

If you win, turn to **240**.

152

The Dwarf congratulates you for guessing correctly. He tells you that you must now progress to the second stage of the test. He reaches for a wicker basket and tells you that a snake is held within it. He tips up the basket and the snake drops on to the floor; it is a cobra, and it rears up in the air ready to strike. The Dwarf tells you that he wishes to test your reactions. Bare-handed, you must grasp the cobra below its head, avoiding its deadly fangs. You crouch down on the floor, tensing yourself for the moment to seize it. Roll two dice. If the total is the same as or less than your SKILL, turn to 55. If the total is greater than your SKILL, turn to 202.

153

The door opens into a small room in which there is a human skull with jewelled eyes resting on top of a marble plinth. A row of loaded crossbows is fixed to the left-hand wall, and two small wooden balls lie on the floor just inside the door. Will you:

Walk into the room and pick up the skull?	Turn to 390
Throw a wooden ball at the skull from the doorway?	Turn to 371
Close the door and continue west, taking the wooden balls with you?	Turn to 74

154

Running down the tunnel, you soon catch up with the Barbarian and tell him that the eastern passage comes to a dead end. He nods his head in silent understanding and sets off towards the west with you at his side. Turn to **22**.

155

The words of her poem flash through your mind: 'When corridor doth water meet, do not make a quick retreat . . .' Of course, it is here that she wants you to dive into the water. Now you must decide what to do. If you wish to dive into the water, turn to **378**. If you would rather walk back down the tunnel, turn to **322**.

156

The small plate slides open easily, and you find yourself peering into a room with a deep pit in the floor behind the door. On the opposite wall there are two iron hooks, on one of which hangs a coil of rope. If you wish to open the door, jump over the pit and take the rope, turn to **208**. If you would rather continue north along the tunnel, turn to **326**.

157

The casket opens easily, and inside there is a black velvet bag containing a large pearl. Add 1 LUCK point. After putting the pearl in your pocket, you press on through the cobwebs. Turn to **310**.

158

You lift the jug to your lips and take a swig of the liquid. It burns so much that you drop the jug and grab your throat in agony. You have swallowed acid! Lose 1 SKILL point and 4 STAMINA points. If you are still alive, turn to **275**.

159

Your reactions are still slow because of the poison in your system, and although you try to jump over the outstretched tongue, your legs let you down. The sticky tongue wraps itself around your leg, flipping you over, and starts to pull you towards the pool. Your sword has slipped out of your hand and you start to panic. If you have a dagger, turn to **294**. If you do not have a dagger, turn to **334**.

160

Your armour and sword weigh you down, but you just manage to land safely on the far edge of the pit. You waste no time and head east. Turn to **237**.

161

You push past the two Leprechauns and head off north, the noise of jeering and laughter ringing in your ears. Further up the tunnel you stop to rest and check your belongings. If you had any gems, they are now gone; the Leprechaun who landed on your back stole them from your backpack. You curse the thieving Leprechauns and set off north again. Turn to 29.

162

Removing the box lid by the light of the tunnel, you find an iron key and a large gem. It is a sapphire. Add 1 LUCK point. Placing the items carefully in your backpack, you set off north once again. Turn to 142.

163

The Dwarf calls down from the balcony, congratulating you on your victory. He throws a sack down into the arena and tells you to relax and regain your strength for the final part of the test. Then he walks off, saying he will return in about ten minutes. You open the sack and find a jug of wine and a cooked chicken. If you wish to eat and drink the Dwarf's offerings, turn to 363. If you would rather just sit down and await his return, turn to 302.

164

As you walk along, droplets of water again start falling from the tunnel ceiling. You see wet footprints, made by the same boots that you followed earlier, heading west. The footprints lead to a closed iron door in the right-hand wall of the tunnel, but do not seem to go any further. If you wish to open the door, turn to **299**. If you would rather keep going west, turn to **83**.

165

There is a slot in the padlock into which you place the coin. Immediately the lock clicks apart, and you are able to unchain the stilts. You place them on your shoulder and once again set off north. Turn to **234**.

166

As you touch the emerald eye of the idol, you hear a creaking sound below you. Looking down, you are shocked to see the two stuffed birds taking flight. Their wings flap in jerky movements, but they are soon above you and look set to attack. Fight the FLYING GUARDIANS one at a time, but reduce your SKILL by 3 during this combat because of your restricted position.

	SKILL	STAMINA
First FLYING GUARDIAN	7	8
Second FLYING GUARDIAN	8	8

If you win, turn to **11**.

167

You swing the grappling iron around your head and hurl it at the beast below. The Pit Fiend's huge jaws snap tight over the grappling iron, then it jerks its head back. Still holding the rope, you are pulled off the wall and tumble to the bottom of the pit. Lose 4 STAMINA points. If you are still alive, turn to **203**.

168

Lifting the latch and pushing the heavy stone door open, you find yourself in a large cavern. The light is dim and murky, but as your eyes begin to adjust, you see that the walls are covered in green algae and running with moisture. The floor is strewn with straw. The atmosphere is warm, damp and fetid, and a soft humming sound fills the air. You step gingerly through the straw towards a corner of the cavern, where there appears to be a shallow pit. Peering warily into the pit, you are disgusted to see a mass of pale writhing worms, some as much as half a metre long. Utterly nauseated, you are about to turn away when you notice that their undulating bodies are swarming round a dagger, its point held fast in a crack in the pit floor. The hilt is cased in black leather studded with opals, and the blade is fashioned from a strange reddish-black burnished metal you have never seen before. You long to touch the dagger, but this would mean plunging your hand in among the writhing worms. Do you reach for the dagger – turn to **94** – or back away in disgust and leave the cavern – turn to **267**?

169

He eyes you suspiciously as you offer him a portion of your Provisions. But hunger overcomes his fear and he crams the food into his mouth. You ask him what he is doing in the tunnels, and he explains that he is a servant of one of the Trialmasters, Baron Sukumvit's appointed controllers of sections of his dungeon. He tells you he would like to escape, but no one is allowed to leave the dungeon in case the secret of its construction is revealed. You tell him that you are a contestant in the Trial of Champions and that you would appreciate any help. Rubbing his chin, he turns to you and says. 'One good turn deserves another. All I can tell you is that in a northern tunnel there is a wooden chair carved in the shape of a demon bird. There is a secret panel in the arm of the chair which contains a potion in a glass phial. It's a Doppelganger Potion. Now I must go about my duties. Good luck. I hope we meet again outside these infernal tunnels.' The man then shuffles off and you continue your journey west. Turn to **109**.

170

As you approach the prostrate figure, you see that it is one of your rivals in the Trial of Champions. It is in fact the Elf, and she is fighting for her life in the bone-crushing grip of an enormous BOA CON-STRICTOR. If you wish to help her, turn to **281**. If you would rather leave her to defend herself and walk back to the tunnel to head north, turn to **192**.

171

The door swings open into a small room, but before you know what is happening, you find yourself falling through thin air – there was a pit behind the door which you did not see. You land heavily at the bottom and wince with pain. Lose 4 STAMINA points. The pit walls are roughly chiselled and have plenty of toe- and finger-holds, so you are able to clamber out quite easily. You curse your own eagerness and tell yourself to be more careful in future when entering rooms. Inside the room you see two iron hooks on the wall opposite the door. A coil of rope is hanging on one of them. You put it in your backpack, jump back over the pit to leave the room and head north. Turn to **326**.

172

Remembering the description of the vile Bloodbeast and the warning about toxic gas rising from its pool, you cover your mouth with your sleeve and step forward with your sword drawn, wary of the Bloodbeast's tongue. As you step round the side of its pool, it rolls forward and flicks out its tongue, but you are ready for it and cleave it with one swipe of your sword. The beast howls in pain and stretches forward frantically, trying to clasp you between its blood-filled jaws. You start hacking at its hideous face in an attempt to pierce its real eyes.

BLOODBEAST   SKILL 12   STAMINA 10

As soon as you win your second Attack Round, turn to **278**.

173

The cool water is refreshing and comes from a source which has been sprinkled with Pixie dust. Add 1 STAMINA point and 2 SKILL points. If you have not done so already, you may either drink from the other fountain – turn to **337** – or continue north – turn to **368**.

174

As you make your way back to the doorway, the buzzing sound increases in intensity, and you look around desperately to discover where it is coming from. Glancing up in the nick of time, you see the huge and grotesque black shape of a GIANT FLY emerging from a recess high up in the cavern wall. As it gets closer, you realize that it is at least one and a half metres long. Its opaque wings vibrate, making the sickening buzzing noise you can hear, and its six black hairy legs are poised to grasp your body. Below its multi-faceted eyes is a long, shiny, black proboscis, which darts in and out venomously. You have stolen the Giant Fly's treasure from her brood of maggots, and you must take the consequences. *Test your Luck.* If you are Lucky, turn to **39**. If you are Unlucky, turn to **350**.

Attached to the collar of one of the Guard Dogs is a metal capsule. You prise off the top and find a small tooth inside. It is a Leprechaun's tooth which will bring you good fortune. Add 2 LUCK points. You put the tooth in your pocket and set off east along the tunnel. Turn to **315**.

176

Treading carefully, you slowly make your way up the steps. You soon reach the top without mishap. Continue along the new tunnel. Turn to **277**.

177

You just have time to hear the Gnome yell, 'Three crowns!', before the lock clicks open. As the heavy door swings slowly outwards, the Gnome rushes towards it, hurling the glass ball at your feet. Green gas escapes from the broken glass, and you try to avoid inhaling it. *Test your Luck*. If you are Lucky, turn to **243**. If you are Unlucky, turn to **103**.

178

The door cannot withstand the furious battering you are giving it. The centre panel cracks and splinters, enabling you to kick a hole in it large enough for you to squeeze through. Wet but happy to have survived your ordeal, you set off north again. Turn to **344**.

179

As you rush towards the Dwarf, he pulls two hand darts from his belt and he throws them at you and Throm, hitting both of you in the leg. You are both instantly paralysed by the poison on the tip of the dart. Lose 2 STAMINA points. As though glued to the floor, you can only watch as the Dwarf retrieves his dart from your thigh. He asks you whether you are willing to enter his contest now. You strain to nod your head. Slowly, the effects of the poison wear off and mobility returns. The Dwarf beckons you to follow him, telling Throm to await his return. He opens a secret door in the chamber wall and you follow him into a small circular room. He closes the door behind you and hands you two bone dice, telling you to throw them on the floor. You roll a six and a two, a total of eight. The Dwarf asks you to roll again, but this time you must predict the total: will it be the same, or higher or lower than eight? If you wish to guess that it will be the same, turn to **290**. If you wish to guess that it will total less than eight, turn to **191**. If you wish to guess that it will total more than eight, turn to **84**.

180

As you make a lunge at the Bloodbeast, you suddenly start to feel faint. The gas rising up from the pool is highly toxic and you slump to the floor unconscious. *Test your Luck*. If you are Lucky, turn to **53**. If you are Unlucky, turn to **272**.

181

The tunnel leads into a marble-floored hall with pillars rising right up to the ceiling. As you cross the floor, your footsteps echo through the hall. The hairs on the back of your neck start to prickle as you sense unseen eyes watching you. Unknown to you, one of your rivals is hiding behind a pillar. It is the NINJA, the deadly assassin dressed in black robes. Without a sound, he steps out from behind the pillar and throws a star-edged disc at your back. Instinctively, an inner voice tells you to duck. *Test your Luck*. If you are Lucky, turn to **312**. If you are Unlucky, turn to **45**.

182

The temperature continues to rise and you find yourself dripping with sweat. As you struggle on, the heat intensifies until it feels like white heat and becomes so unbearable that you begin to pass out. If you drank the liquid from the bamboo pipe, turn to **25**. If you did not stop to drink, turn to **242**.

183

You climb on to your stilts and take a few tentative steps across the floor. Your confidence grows, and you soon feel able to tackle the walk across the slime. Smoke rises from the base of the stilts as the slime starts to burn them away. You plod stolidly on and finally reach firm ground again. Unfortunately, the stilts are still covered in slime and you are forced to dump them. Setting off north, you come to a junction. If you wish to go west, turn to **386**. If you wish to continue north, turn to **218**.

184

The Barbarian, who tells you he is called Throm, ties the rope around his waist, giving you the free end. As he lights the torch, you see a look of distrust in his eyes. Slowly, he climbs over the edge of the pit while you brace yourself and take the strain of the rope. As you lower him little by little, you see the smooth sides of the pit illuminated by Throm's torch. He finally reaches the bottom and calls up to you, saying that there is another tunnel running north. He tells you to secure the rope around a rock protruding from the edge of the pit and lower yourself to the bottom. If you wish to stay with the Barbarian and head north down the lower tunnel, turn to **323**. If you wish to abandon him by jumping over the pit to head west, turn to **149**.

185

The Troglodytes are too involved in their tribal dancing to hear the clatter of your sword, and you crawl past. When you think you are far enough away, you stand up and run across the cavern floor. Ahead you see an underground river running east to west through the cavern with a wooden bridge crossing over it. Hearing a noise, you glance back and realize you have been spotted. The Troglodytes are chasing you. If you wish to run over the bridge, turn to **318**. If you wish to dive into the river, turn to **47**.

186

Slowly and carefully, you begin to climb the idol. You are about to grab hold of its large ear when suddenly your foot slips. *Test your Luck*. If you are Lucky, turn to **260**. If you are Unlucky, turn to **358**.

187

The tunnel bends sharply to the right, and around the corner you see a little old man with a long beard, cowering behind a large wicker basket. The basket is tied to a rope, the other end of which disappears into the ceiling. The old man sounds very worried as he says, 'Do not attack me, stranger. I pose no threat to you. I am here simply to help you. If you would be so kind as to offer me some sort of remuneration, I will gladly haul you up in the basket to the upper level. And believe me, that is where you ought to be.' If you wish to give the man something from your backpack for his services, turn to **360**. If you would rather walk past him down the tunnel, turn to **280**.

188

The tunnel starts to slope downwards and finally comes to an end at a deep pool enclosed by the tunnel wall. If you can remember the spirit girl's poem, turn to **155**. If you have not seen the spirit girl, turn to **224**.

189

The Orc's morning star sinks agonizingly into your left thigh. Lose 3 STAMINA points. You stagger backwards, but manage to regain your balance in time to defend yourself. Fortunately, the tunnel is too narrow for both Orcs to attack you at once. Fight them one at a time.

	SKILL	STAMINA
First ORC	5	5
Second ORC	6	4

If you win, turn to **257**.

190

Your body vibrates wildly and you are unable to stop yourself passing out. Lose 3 STAMINA points. If you are still alive, turn to **50**.

191

Roll two dice. If the total is less than eight, turn to **152**. If the total is eight or higher, turn to **121**.

192

Walking along the tunnel, you notice an iron grille in the floor. If you wish to stop and lift it up, turn to **120**. If you prefer to keep walking, turn to **292**.

193

The acid burns through your stomach wall, eating its way into your vital organs. You collapse unconscious, never to recover. Your adventure ends here.

194

On a stone ledge in the tunnel wall you see two dusty leather-bound books. Throm grunts his contempt for the written word, urging you to leave the books and hurry on. Will you:

Open the red leather book?	Turn to **52**
Open the black leather book?	Turn to **138**
Continue north along the tunnel?	Turn to **369**

195

You draw your sword and rush towards the old man. He raises his left arm and suddenly you hit and bounce off an invisible shield. 'Do not be foolish, my powers are great,' the old man says calmly. 'If you do not believe me, watch this.' From out of nowhere a flying fist appears, which smashes into your face before you can duck. Lose 1 STAMINA point. You shake your head and rub your jaw. You appear to have no alternative but to try to answer his question. Turn to **382**.

196

You raise your shield in front of you just in time to protect yourself from a volley of spikes released from the Manticore's tail and aimed straight at your heart. They sink into your shield and you remain unharmed. Swiftly you draw your sword and advance on the Manticore.

MANTICORE   SKILL 11   STAMINA 11

If you win, turn to **364**.

197

Mercifully, the temperature now starts to drop rapidly, and soon it feels almost cool again. On the left-hand side of the tunnel is a closed door. It has a small iron plate in it, which might possibly slide open. Will you:

Try to open the door?	Turn to **171**
Try to slide the iron plate?	Turn to **156**
Continue north up the tunnel?	Turn to **326**

198

Once the gas has cleared, you walk back to the chest and look inside. There is a pendant chain lying in the bottom of it, but somebody has already removed the stone from its setting. This annoys you so much that you throw the chain on to the floor and storm out of the room and up the tunnel. Turn to **230**.

199

The crossbow bolts are far too many to evade. Roll one die to determine the number of bolts that sink into your body, and lose 2 STAMINA points for each one. If you are still alive, you must rest here a long time to recover from your wounds. Lose 1 LUCK point. When you eventually feel strong enough to carry on, you leave the room and continue west along the tunnel. Turn to **74**.

200

The door opens into a small room with a straw-covered floor. In the centre of the room there is a large draped cage standing some two metres high. There is a cord fixed to the top of the drape which runs up through an iron ring in the ceiling and hangs down to the floor. If you wish to pull the drape up, turn to **321**. If you would prefer to leave the room and head north along the tunnel, turn to **316**.

201

You search through the cupboards and boxes in Ivy's room, but you find nothing except for an old bone. A door lies in the east wall of the chamber and you decide to leave, taking the old bone with you if you wish. You now find yourself standing at the end of another tunnel. Turn to **305**.

202

The cobra's reactions are quicker than yours, and its hooded head shoots forward to bite you. *Test your Luck.* If you are Lucky, turn to **18**. If you are Unlucky, turn to **42**.

203

You stagger to your feet and draw your sword. You are only just in time, for the fearsome beast is closing in on you fast. This is going to be one of the toughest fights of your life.

PIT FIEND   SKILL 12   STAMINA 15

If you win, turn to **258**.

204

There is an unseen pressure plate on top of the plinth, and as soon as the skull is put back on it, the device is sprung. Immediately the crossbows release a shower of bolts across the room. *Test your Luck*. If you are Lucky, turn to **131**. If you are Unlucky, turn to **199**.

205

Running after the Leprechauns, you hear more laughter, only now it is behind you. You look round and see six more Leprechauns emerging from behind a hidden door in the tunnel wall. Suddenly, yet another Leprechaun drops on your back from a ledge fixed to the ceiling. Shaking him off your back, you draw your sword, whereupon the Leprechauns laugh even louder. If you wish to attack them, turn to **306**. If you would rather try to walk past them, turn to **161**.

206

The stalactites continue to fall all around you, but you haven't enough strength to do more than crawl towards the archway. Suddenly you feel an arm around your waist picking you up, and realize in your semi-conscious state that Throm is carrying you. He lays you down in the safety of the tunnel and tends your wounds. You decide to eat some of your Provisions to help regain your strength, and you also give one portion to Throm in gratitude for his rescuing you. He apologizes for starting the rock-fall and offers you his hand to shake. Despite the pain, you manage a smile and shake his hand. When you have finally recovered, you stand up and head east, with Throm leading the way. Turn to **60**.

207

You take off your shirt and tear it in half. You wrap a piece around each foot to give yourself some sort of protection against the corrosive slime, and dash across it in giant leaps. On the firm ground beyond the slime, you frantically try to rip the burning shirt off your feet with your sword. However, some of the slime has eaten its way through to your ankle. Lose 3 STAMINA points. Setting off north again, you come to a junction. If you wish to go west, turn to **386**. If you wish to continue north, turn to **218**.

208

The door swings open into the room, and you step back and jump over the pit. You put the rope in your backpack and jump back over the pit to leave the room and head north. Turn to **326**.

209

You are dismayed to find that not only are all your remaining Provisions saturated and inedible, but one of the treasures you found is missing. Cross off one item on your Equipment List, or one of your jewels or potions. You carefully repack your remaining possessions and set off north again. Turn to **356**.

210

You enter a room in which a man in tattered clothing is standing chained to the wall by his left arm. You see that his right hand is missing and realize that his must be the hand nailed to the door. Pleading for mercy, he cowers back from you as far as his chains will allow. If you wish to cut him free from his chains, turn to **27**. If you would rather leave the room to head north, turn to **78**.

211

You manage to free yourself from Ivy's grip and draw your sword. Picking up a broken stool as a weapon, she advances towards you.

IVY   SKILL 9   STAMINA 9

If you win, turn to **201**.

212

Gripping the rope firmly, you step back to take a running jump. However, in the dim light you do not notice that someone has cut the rope almost in two just a little way above the section you are holding. As you swing out across the pit it suddenly breaks, and you scream with fear as you plunge headlong to the depths below. Turn to **285**.

213

The tunnel soon divides into two. You hear a buzzing sound coming from the western branch. If you wish to walk west to investigate who or what is making the noise, turn to **108**. If you would rather continue north, turn to **14**.

214

Walking along, you see a red line painted across the tunnel floor and notice a sign on the wall which reads: 'No weapons beyond this point'. If you wish to abandon any weapons before continuing north, turn to **389**. If you would rather ignore the notice and carry on north, turn to **181**.

215

Your sword easily pierces the thin outer casing of the giant spore ball. A thick brown cloud of spores bursts out of the ball and envelops you. Some of the spores stick to your skin and start to itch terribly. Great lumps come up on your face and arms, and your skin feels as if it is on fire. Lose 2 STAMINA points. Frantically scratching your itching lumps, you step over the now deflated spore ball and head east. Turn to **13**.

216

Recognizing the snake-like head of the Medusa, you close your eyes to avoid her deadly stare that would turn you to stone. If you wish to enter her cage with your eyes closed to dispose of her with your sword, turn to **308**. If you would rather retreat out of the room with your eyes closed to continue north, turn to **316**.

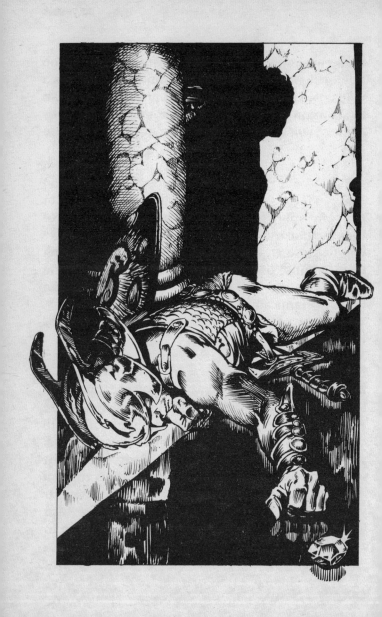

217

The passage slowly starts to climb, leading you relentlessly northwards. You do not come across a single junction. There are no doorways or even an alcove to investigate, and you become less guarded as you plod on. After a while you become so non-chalant that you fail to notice a thin tripwire stretched low across the passage. It is only when your foot catches it and you hear a distant rumble that you realize your mistake. The rumbling sound swells to an almost deafening level, and suddenly out of the gloom of the tunnel ahead you see a massive boulder rolling towards you, gathering speed with every second. Dropping your shield if you have one (lose 1 SKILL point), you turn to flee the oncoming boulder. Turn to 36.

218

You soon arrive at a double door in the left-hand wall. You listen at the door but hear nothing. You try the handle, it turns and you open the left door slightly and peer through the crack. An armed warrior is lying face down on the floor of a bare room with smooth walls and a low ceiling. He is presumably dead, for he makes no movement even when you call out to him. A large jewel, perhaps a diamond, lies just beyond his outstretched arm. If you wish to enter the room and take the jewel, turn to 65. If you would rather continue north, turn to 252.

219

The pain in your lungs forces you to rise to the surface for air. Unfortunately, one of the Troglodytes sees you and yells to his comrades. You watch helplessly as the bowmen take aim, and a hail of arrows falls on you with fatal impact. Your lifeless body floats down-river, down into the hidden depths of the mountain.

220

A dull 'bong' sounds from the bell like a death toll. Everything around you starts to vibrate, and you grit your teeth as your head too starts to shudder. Your whole body is trembling and you fall to the floor. You quiver and shake, writhing convulsively on the floor as the vibrations intensify. Lose 2 SKILL points and 2 STAMINA points. You search desperately for a way of stopping the bell. Will you:

Scream as loud as you can?	Turn to **61**
Try to deaden the bell with your boot?	Turn to **346**

221

The tunnel leads into a damp, high-ceilinged cavern with a rock-strewn floor. Long dripping teeth-like stalactites hang down threateningly, their constant dripping creating milky pools on the floor. The tunnel carries on through an archway carved in the shape of a demonic mouth. If you wish to search the chamber, turn to **374**. If you would rather head straight for the archway, turn to **60**.

222

You recognize the beast – it is a MANTICORE. Taking heed of the poem's warning, you watch out for its tail which sprouts a profusion of sharp spikes, thick and hard as iron bolts, at its tip. If you have a shield, turn to **196**. If you are not carrying a shield, turn to **6**.

223

You step confidently on to the first pole and stride across to the next. As you land on the third pole, it immediately releases a shower of sharp splinters, each several centimetres long. Lose 2 LUCK points. They fly out in all directions at great speed, and you cannot avoid being hit. Roll two dice for the number of splinters that sink into your flesh. Each one reduces your STAMINA by one point. If you are still alive, you manage to scramble over the remaining poles and sit down to the painful task of removing the splinters from your body. After resting for a while, you set off east again. Turn to **313**.

224

There does not appear to be any way of travelling further north. You turn around and walk back down the tunnel, passing the wooden chair. You soon arrive at the junction and turn right to head west. Turn to **43**.

225

You react quickly and manage to cleave the Blood-beast's outstretched tongue with one swipe of your blade. The beast screams in pain and hurls itself forward to try and clasp you between its blood-filled jaws. This will be a fight to the death.

BLOODBEAST   SKILL 12   STAMINA 10

As soon as you win your first Attack Round, *Test your Luck*. If you are Lucky, turn to **97**. If you are Unlucky, turn to **21**.

226

The meat contains herbs which will increase your strength. Add 3 to your STAMINA score. You may either walk over to the alcove if you have not done so already – turn to **41** – or leave the chamber to continue west – turn to **83**.

227

Still smiling, the old man looks at you. 'Wrong,' he says quietly. Turn to **85**.

228

You reach down into the hole. Suddenly your blood runs cold as you feel something warm and sticky wrapping itself around your arm. You manage to pull your arm out of the hole, but a hideous tentacled limb with unbelievably strong suckers is clinging to your arm. By the time you manage to cut yourself free, your arm is trembling with pain. *Test your Luck*. If you are Lucky, turn to **150**. If you are Unlucky, turn to **33**.

229

As soon as your head goes under the blue light, you hear the sound of muffled voices. The faces are no longer laughing, but have changed their expressions to ones of despair and anguish. A young girl's sad face hovers in front of you, and she begins to whisper a poem. Transfixed you listen intently, believing that she has a special message for you as she recites:

> 'When corridor doth water meet,
> Do not make a quick retreat.
> Take a breath and jump deep in
> If your Trial you hope to win.'

Memorizing the spirit girl's poem, you step through the shaft of light and quickly head on north. Turn to **107**.

230

The tunnel starts to widen, and ahead you see it open into a huge cavern from where you can hear the sound of many high-pitched voices. You creep up to the entrance and take a look inside. There are about twenty tiny people with long noses and ears running in a circle around a large golden effigy. Will you:

Walk up and talk to them?	Turn to **88**
Try to creep past them?	Turn to **5**
Drink a Doppelganger Potion (if you have one)?	Turn to **385**

231

You find a pool behind the dead Hobgoblins and take great gulps of the cool water as fast as you can. This neutralizes the acid and slowly you begin to recover. Still in pain, you stand up and set off north. Turn to **110**.

232

If you are unarmed, turn to **286**. If you still have your weapons, turn to **320**.

233

You break off a large piece of the mushroom and bite into it eagerly. Immediately your stomach feels bloated and you can even see it beginning to bulge below your belt. Your whole body starts to expand, bursting out of your clothes with a loud ripping sound. You grow bigger and bigger, and soon your face is pressed against the ceiling. The mushrooms you have eaten are much sought after by wizards for their growth potions, but to you they spell doom. You are too large ever to leave the cellar, and your adventure ends here.

234

A little farther on you come to a section of the tunnel which is covered with thick green slime. It looks threatening, so you decide to test it first with a piece of cloth. The slime's corrosive jelly burns the cloth instantly, leaving no trace. If you are carrying a pair of stilts, turn to **183**. If you do not have them, turn to **207**.

235

You have no time to react before the dart thuds into your thigh. Lose 2 STAMINA points. If you are still alive, turn to **73**.

236

The fist retracts and prepares to strike again. With your free hand you draw your sword and try to cut the handle of the door. Although you do not recognize it, you are being attacked by the fluid form of an IMITATOR.

IMITATOR   SKILL 9   STAMINA 8

As soon as you win your first Attack Round, turn to **314**.

237

The tunnel makes a sudden left turn and continues north for as far as you can see. You soon arrive at a closed wooden door in the left-hand wall. If you wish to open the door, turn to **12**. If you would rather keep going north, turn to **100**.

238

As you fall, you manage to grab the rope with your hands. Slowly you haul yourself over to the far side and scramble up on to the floor. You lift the helmet off the pole and put it on your head. It has been made by a highly skilled ironsmith. Add 1 SKILL point. Not wishing to risk walking back across the tightrope, you decide to crawl along it. Safely back on firm ground, you step through the archway and head north up the tunnel. Turn to **291**.

239

Not much farther down the tunnel you come to a closed door on your left. Putting your ear to the door, you listen intently but hear nothing. If you wish to open the door, turn to **102**. If you wish to keep walking north, turn to **344**.

240

You look down and see the crumpled bodies of the two Flying Guardians lying motionless on the floor. You start to prise out the idol's emerald eye with the tip of your sword. At last it comes free and you are surprised by its weight when it falls into your hand. Hoping it may be of use later, you put it in your backpack. If you now wish to prise out the right eye, turn to **34**. If you would rather climb down the idol, turn to **89**.

241

A brown velvet curtain is draped over an archway in the eastern wall of the tunnel. If you wish to pull back the curtain and walk through the archway, turn to **393**. If you would rather continue north, turn to **291**.

242

You shake your head, trying desperately to stop yourself from blacking out, but the heat is too much for you and you fall unconscious to the floor. Roll two dice. If the total is the same as or less than your SKILL, turn to **48**. If the total is greater than your SKILL, turn to **366**.

243

Covering your nose and mouth with your hand to avoid breathing in the gas, you follow the Gnome through the open door. You enter another tunnel, at the end of which is the welcome sight of daylight. Much to your surprise, you see the Gnome lying dead halfway down the tunnel. A crossbow bolt protrudes from the side of his head. The Gnome, in his bid for freedom, has fallen foul of Baron Sukumvit's final trap. You walk past him and out into brilliant sunshine. Turn to **400**.

244

He takes your Gold Piece and tells you that in a northern tunnel there is a wooden chair carved in the shape of a demon bird. In the arm of the chair is a secret panel which contains a potion in a glass phial. 'It's a Doppelganger Potion, if I remember right. Good luck. I hope we meet again outside these infernal tunnels.' The man shuffles off and you continue your journey. Turn to **109**.

245

You have no choice but to open the door, as the wall is too smooth to climb. Taking a deep breath, you turn the handle and enter a sand-covered pit. There, standing some ten metres tall on its huge hind legs in front of large double doors in the opposite wall, is an enormous dinosaur-like monster. It has a tough, mottled green hide and a mouth lined with razor-sharp teeth. Its jaws open and close with bone-snapping power, and even you cannot help trembling as you approach it with your sword drawn.

PIT FIEND   SKILL 12   STAMINA 15

If you win, turn to **258**.

246

Despite being as careful as possible, your leg brushes against one of the poles. It immediately releases a shower of sharp splinters, each several centimetres long. Lose 2 LUCK points. They fly out at great speed and in all directions, and you cannot avoid being hit. Roll two dice for the number of splinters that sink into your flesh. Each splinter reduces your STAMINA by one point. If you are still alive, you sit down to the painful task of removing the splinters from your body before setting off east. Turn to **313**.

247

The beast before you is the dreaded MANTICORE. The tip of its tail sprouts a profusion of sharp spikes, thick and hard as iron bolts. Suddenly it flicks its tail, sending a volley of spikes flying towards you. Roll one die. This is the number of spikes that sink into your body. Lose 2 STAMINA points for each spike. If you are still alive, you stagger forward to attack the Manticore with your sword before it has time to unleash any more of its deadly spikes.

MANTICORE   SKILL 11   STAMINA 11

If you win, turn to **364**.

248

The doors open into a tunnel running north. You close the doors behind you and set off once again. Turn to **214**.

249

You just have time to hear the Gnome say, 'One crown and two skulls', before a white bolt of energy shoots out from the lock into your chest, knocking you unconscious. Roll one die, add 1 to the number and reduce your STAMINA by the total. If you are still alive, you come to and are told by the Gnome to try again. You know you placed one gem in the correct slot, but which one? You sigh and tentatively try a new combination.

A	B	C	
Emerald	Diamond	Sapphire	Turn to **16**
Diamond	Sapphire	Emerald	Turn to **392**
Sapphire	Emerald	Diamond	Turn to **177**
Emerald	Sapphire	Diamond	Turn to **287**
Diamond	Emerald	Sapphire	Turn to **132**
Sapphire	Diamond	Emerald	Turn to **249**

250

As you run for the door, the old man calls out behind you, 'Do not run, nobody escapes me. Stop, or I shall turn you to stone this instant!' Will you:

Keep on running?	Turn to **44**
Turn to attack him with your sword?	Turn to **195**
Tell him you will answer his question?	Turn to **382**

251

Once again the mysterious voice calls out, only this time, to your great surprise, in a far less threatening tone, 'Good, my master likes those who show spirit. Take this gift to help you. It will grant you one wish, but one wish only. Farewell.' A gold ring magically appears out of nowhere and lands at your feet with a gentle tinkle. You pick it up and put it on one of your fingers. The door opens and you step back into the tunnel to continue north. Turn to **344**.

252

The tunnel continues north for quite a distance before coming to a dead end. The mouth of a chute protrudes from the western wall, and it appears to be the only alternative to turning back. You decide to risk it and climb into the chute. You slide gently down and emerge into a room, landing on your back. Turn to **90**.

253

You take the bone out of your backpack and throw it down the stairs. The barking grows louder, changing to snarls and growls when the bone lands on the floor. You walk slowly down the steps with your sword drawn and see two huge black GUARD DOGS fighting over the bone. You run quickly past them and on down the tunnel. Turn to **315**.

254

You draw your sword and advance slowly towards the huge, slimy Rock Grub.

ROCK GRUB   SKILL 7   STAMINA 11

If you win, turn to **76**. You may *Escape* after two Attack Rounds by running west down the tunnel. Turn to **117**.

255

As you run round the narrow path, you suddenly start to feel dizzy. The gas from the pool is taking effect: your vision starts to blur and you lose your balance. You are only half aware of the Bloodbeast's tongue as it wraps itself around your leg and drags you into the pool of slime. After being predigested by the vile slime, the hideous Bloodbeast will consume you at its leisure.

256

Remembering the old man's advice, you search the arm of the chair for a secret panel. You find an almost invisible crack in the arm, which you start to press and squeeze. Suddenly a tiny panel springs out of the arm and you see a glass phial lying in a cavity. You pick it out and read the label: 'Doppelganger Potion – one dose only. This liquid will make you assume the shape of any nearby living being.' You place the strange potion in your backpack and continue north. Turn to **188**.

257

Inside one of the Orcs' pockets you find one Gold Piece and a hollow wooden tube. You put your findings in your backpack and set off west. Turn to 164.

258

You are exhausted and sit down for a rest on the tail of the dead beast. Looking down at your feet, you suddenly notice an iron ring poking up through the sand. If you wish to pull the ring, turn to 95. If you would rather leave the pit via the double doors, turn to 248.

259

Ignoring the pain, you run on. Ahead you see an underground river running east to west through the cavern, with a wooden bridge crossing over it. You look behind and see the Troglodytes in hot pursuit. If you wish to run over the bridge, turn to 318. If you wish to dive into the river, turn to 47.

260

You just manage to grab the idol's earlobe and regain your footing. You scramble over its face and sit down on the bridge of its nose. You draw your sword and consider which jewelled eye to prise out first. If you wish to prise out the left eye, turn to 166. If you wish to prise out the right eye, turn to 140.

261

Despite all your efforts, you cannot get the lasso off the idol's neck. Finally you give up and abandon it to whoever may come after you. There is nothing else of interest in the cavern, so you walk over to the northern wall and enter the tunnel. Turn to **239**.

262

The door opens into another tunnel running north. Ahead you see two stone fountains, one on either side of the tunnel, carved in the shape of cherubs. Water spouts from their mouths and cascades into small bowls at their feet. Will you:

Drink at the fountain on your left?	Turn to **337**
Drink at the fountain on your right?	Turn to **173**
Continue your walk north?	Turn to **368**

263

The door opens into another tunnel. Walking west, you soon arrive at a door in the north wall. If you wish to open the door, turn to **153**. If you would rather continue west, turn to **74**.

264

Ahead in the dim light you see two HOBGOBLINS fighting, punching and kicking each other furiously. There is a leather bag lying on the floor, and it seems to be this that they are fighting over. Will you:

Try to talk to them?	Turn to 130
Attack them with your sword?	Turn to 51
Try to slip by them unnoticed?	Turn to 355

265

You rub your magic ring and wish for the Mirror Demon to be transported back to its own world, never to return. Still advancing towards you, it starts to shimmer and fade away. Then it vanishes completely, and you are able to continue your quest north. Turn to 122.

266

You search through the cupboards and boxes in Ivy's room, but you find nothing except an old bone, which you may take with you if you wish. Leaving the chamber by the east door, you now find yourself standing at the end of another tunnel. Turn to 305.

267

The tunnel ends shortly at a junction. Looking left and right, you see a narrow passage disappearing into the dim distance. If you wish to head west, turn to 352. If you wish to go east, turn to 68.

268

You leap forward and try to grab the leader to use as a hostage. However, the Troglodytes are ready for your move, and six of their bowmen immediately shoot their arrows at you. Their aim is deadly accurate and all six arrows find their mark. Lifeless, you fall to the floor. The Troglodytes have ended your journey abruptly.

269

You empty the contents of the jar into your hand and apply them to your wounds. Their healing powers take immediate effect and you feel yourself growing stronger. Add 3 STAMINA points. If you have not done so already, you may either eat the rice and drink the water – turn to **330** – or leave the hall, taking just the diamond with you – turn to **127**.

270

The lid of the box lifts off easily. Inside you find two Gold Pieces and a note written on a small piece of parchment addressed to you. After placing the gold in your pocket, you read the message, which says: 'Well done. At least you have the sense to stop and take advantage of the token aid given to you. Now I can advise you that you will need to find and use several items if you hope to pass triumphantly through my Deathtrap Dungeon. Signed Sukum-vit.' Memorizing the advice on the note, you tear it into tiny pieces and continue north along the tunnel. Turn to **66**.

271

Just as you are about to release the shield and throw it over the pit, it slips from your fingers and rolls away. You are unable to catch it before it falls over the edge of the pit, clattering down its sides to the bottom. The loss of your shield reduces your fighting ability – lose one SKILL point. Cursing your own clumsiness, you step forward, leap across the pit and land safely on the other side. You waste no time but head off east. Turn to **237**.

272

Although the Bloodbeast is too bulbous and heavy to climb out of its pool, its long tongue stretches and wraps itself around your leg. Still unconscious, you are dragged into its pool of slime. After being pre-digested by the vile slime, the hideous Bloodbeast will consume you at its leisure.

273

The wooden ball smashes into the skull, knocking it off the plinth and on to the floor. Much to your surprise, the crossbows do not release their deadly bolts. You step into the room cautiously and pick the skull up off the floor. You recognize the yellow jewelled eyes as topaz, and eagerly pluck them from their sockets. You put them in your backpack, wondering whether or not a trap still awaits you in the room. Will you:

Get down on all fours and crawl out of the room holding the skull?	Turn to **15**
Replace the skull on the plinth before leaving the room?	Turn to **204**

274

You step nervously on to the rope, not daring to look down. Halfway across, you start to panic and lose your footing. Roll two dice. If the total is the same as or less than your SKILL, turn to **238**. If the total is higher than your SKILL, turn to **359**.

275

Thick smoke rises up from the floor where the acid has fallen from the broken jug. You crawl along the floor desperately trying to find drinkable water in the shallow pools of the dripping tunnel. *Test your Luck*. If you are Lucky, turn to **231**. If you are Unlucky, turn to **309**.

276

As you try to charge down the door with your shoulder, you hear the shrieking voices of the Troglodytes coming down the tunnel. You are trapped and draw your sword. The Troglodytes approach you, their bows drawn, and a hail of arrows strikes you with fatal impact. Your lifeless body slumps to the ground in the depths of Death-trap Dungeon.

277

The tunnel takes a sharp right turn and then, a hundred metres ahead, comes to a junction. Looking left, you see two bodies lying on the floor. You decide to go and investigate. Turn to **338**.

278

Your blade strikes one of the Bloodbeast's real eyes with devastating effect. It slumps back into its pool, thrashing about in a frenzy. You seize your opportunity and run round the side of the pool to the tunnel exit. Turn to **134**.

279

You arrive at a junction in the tunnel. A new branch leads west, but the wet footprints you have been following continue north. You decide to keep following the footprints. Turn to **32**.

280

The tunnel continues east for quite a long way before reaching a junction. The walls, ceiling and floor of the tunnel leading south are covered with a thick green slime. You decide it would be safer to head north. Turn to **218**.

281

With one swipe of your trusty blade you behead the Boa Constrictor. You uncoil its massive body from around the Elf and try to resuscitate her. Her eyes open a little, but you can see that there is no hope. She looks at you and smiles, then says in a whisper, 'Thank you. I know it's too late for me, but I will tell you what I have learned. Your way out lies ahead, but you need gems to unlock the final door. One of them is a diamond, but I do not know what the others are. Alas, I have not found a diamond, but would urge you to look for one. Good luck.' Her eyes close and she slumps down on to the cold floor. You watch sadly as she breathes her last. Knowing she would not mind, you take two of her daggers and search her leather backpack. Inside you find some unleavened bread, a mirror and a bone charm in the shape of a monkey. If you wish to eat the bread, turn to **399**. If you would rather just take the mirror and charm and return to the tunnel to head north, turn to **192**.

282

The tunnel soon ends at a junction. Standing there alone and wondering which way to go is one of your rivals. It is one of the Barbarians. You call out to him, but at first he does not answer, he merely stares at you coldly, his hands firmly gripping his axe. You walk up to him and ask which way he is heading. He grunts his reply, saying that he is going west, and you may go with him if you wish. If you would like to head west with the Barbarian, turn to **22**. If you would rather decline his offer and head east alone, turn to **388**.

283

You have to squeeze yourself deep into the crack to conceal yourself completely. From this cramped position you are unable to see the owner of the feet that shuffle slowly by. A minute later all is quiet again, so you pull yourself back out into the tunnel and head west. Turn to **109**.

284

Have you drunk a potion found in a black leather book? If you have, turn to **398**. If you have not swallowed this potion, turn to **57**.

285

You land heavily on your back, but luckily your backpack cushions your fall. Lose 1 SKILL point and 2 STAMINA points. The darkness is almost pitch black at the bottom of the pit, and you crawl along the floor, groping in front of you. Suddenly your hand touches something cold, hard and smooth. The object is small and round, but you cannot figure out what it is. You place it in your backpack, hoping to see what it is once out of the pit. You continue to crawl forward and soon reach the pit wall. It is too smooth to climb, and you have to cut hand- and toe-holds in it with your sword. This takes a long time, but finally you climb out of the pit on the east side. You immediately check out the object in your backpack, and discover that you have found an orb of blood-red ruby. You are absolutely delighted and head off east in high spirits, whistling softly under your breath. Turn to **237**.

286

It was obviously a mistake to drop your weapons earlier, but at least you can now take those of the dead Ninja. You select one of his long knives and his long curved sword. Its steel cutting edge is exceptionally hard, and you cannot help but admire its awesome beauty. Add 4 SKILL points and turn to **320**.

287

You just have time to hear the Gnome say, 'One crown and two skulls', before a white bolt of energy shoots out from the lock into your chest, knocking you unconscious. Roll one die, add 1 to the number and reduce your STAMINA by the total. If you are still alive, you come to and are told by the Gnome to try again. You know you placed one gem in the correct slot, but which one? You sigh and tentatively try a new combination.

A	B	C	
Emerald	Diamond	Sapphire	Turn to **16**
Diamond	Sapphire	Emerald	Turn to **392**
Sapphire	Emerald	Diamond	Turn to **177**
Emerald	Sapphire	Diamond	Turn to **287**
Diamond	Emerald	Sapphire	Turn to **132**
Sapphire	Diamond	Emerald	Turn to **249**

288

You look to your left and see Throm standing over the Cave Troll he has slain. Blood is pouring out from a deep cut in his shoulder, but it does not seem to worry him. You search the bodies of the Cave Trolls, but find nothing apart from a bone ring on a leather cord hanging round the neck of one of them. The ring is engraved with a symbol which Throm recognizes. He explains that it must have belonged to druids of the north and that an ancient talisman such as this will increase your powers if your body is able to accept it. Throm will not touch it, and advises you to leave it well alone. If you wish to put the ring on, turn to **64**. If you would rather continue east with Throm, turn to **221**.

289

The drape rises to the top of the cage and there, to your horror, you see the face of an aged woman whose hair is a mass of seething snakes. It is the dreaded MEDUSA! *Test your Luck*. If you are Lucky, turn to **216**. If you are Unlucky, turn to **19**.

290

Roll two dice. If the total is eight, turn to **152**. If the total is any number other than eight, turn to **121**.

291

The tunnel continues north a long way before turning sharp right. Around the corner you come to a dead end. Only the mouth of a wooden chute in the wall offers any hope of further progress. You decide to take a chance and climb into the chute. You slide gently down and emerge into a room, landing on your back. Turn to **90**.

292

A door comes into view in the left-hand wall of the tunnel. You listen carefully at the door but hear nothing. The door is not locked and the handle turns easily. If you wish to open the door, turn to **93**. If you would rather keep walking along the tunnel, turn to **230**.

293

Following the three sets of wet footprints along the west passage of the tunnel, you soon arrive at a junction. If you wish to continue west, following two sets of footprints, turn to **137**. If you wish to head north, following the third set of footprints, turn to **387**.

294

You pull the dagger from your belt with your free hand and hack at the Bloodbeast's tongue. The beast screams in pain and rolls forward as far as it can to try and clasp you between its blood-filled jaws. You must fight it from the floor with your dagger. Reduce your SKILL by 2 during this combat because you are not fighting with your sword.

BLOODBEAST   SKILL 12   STAMINA 10

As soon as you win your first Attack Round, *Test your Luck*. If you are Lucky, turn to **97**. If you are Unlucky, turn to **21**.

295

Running towards the archway, you stumble over a rock and lose your footing. You land sprawled on the floor, and before you have time to get up again, a stalactite crashes down on top of you, its pointed tip piercing your leg. Lose 5 STAMINA points. If you are still alive, turn to **206**.

296

Ahead you see that the tunnel turns a corner, beyond which it continues north. You stop before the corner, startled by the sound of high-pitched voices whispering and sniggering. If you wish to draw your sword and look round the corner, turn to **49**. If you would rather walk back to the junction to head north, turn to **241**.

297

Losing your hard-earned possessions is becoming a bit of a problem. Lose 1 LUCK point. Without even pausing to thank you, Ivy pushes you out of her chamber through a door in the east wall, and you find yourself standing at the end of another tunnel. Turn to **305**.

298

You see a backpack propped up against the tunnel wall. You wonder if it belongs to one of your rivals. If you wish to look inside the backpack, turn to **304**. If you would rather continue north, turn to **279**.

299

The door opens into a large chamber, where you are shocked to see one of your rivals, who has obviously met a sudden gory death. It is one of the Barbarians, and he is impaled on several long iron spikes which are fixed to a frame that has sprung out of the floor. A lot of rubbish and debris litters the floor, concealing a hidden trip-wire which he must have stepped on and thus released the spiked frame. In the far wall is an alcove, in which you can see a silver goblet standing on a small wooden table. Will you:

Walk over to search the Barbarian?   Turn to **126**
Walk towards the alcove?   Turn to **41**
Close the door and continue west?   Turn to **83**

300

You swing your sword against the mirror with all your might, but to no effect: the mirror does not break, and the Mirror Demon keeps advancing. If you wish to try and smash the mirror again, turn to **141**. If you would rather attack the Mirror Demon instead, turn to **327**.

301

The pipe is wet and slimy, but you crawl on into the dank darkness, slithering and sliding as you go. Suddenly your hand touches something hard and square which feels as if it is made of wood. It rattles as you shake it, and you decide you must be holding a box. If you wish to crawl back out of the pipe and examine your find, turn to **162**. If you would rather press on further down the pipe, taking the box with you to examine later, turn to **4**.

302

After about twenty minutes the Dwarf reappears on the balcony. He calls down to you, saying, 'Well, I do have an interesting problem on my hands. Prepare to fight your next opponent.' The wooden door rises once again and you are surprised to see a familiar face. It is Throm! He is cut and badly bruised, and doesn't seem to recognize you. He is clearly delirious as he staggers forward with his axe raised to attack you. The Dwarf laughs and says, 'The cobra bit him, but he has the strength of an ox and managed to carry on, even though most men would have died. Now you must fight him to decide finally which of you will continue the Trial of Champions.' You shout abuse at the Dwarf, protesting against the cruelty of such a contest. He merely laughs, and you have no option but to defend yourself against poor Throm.

THROM   SKILL 10   STAMINA 12

Despite his wounds, Throm is immensely strong. If you win, turn to **379**.

303

With your free hand, you reach into your backpack and take out the jug. Uncorking it with your teeth, you pour the acid over the door, which is in fact the fluid form of an IMITATOR. A jet of smoke rises from it with a loud hissing sound as the acid immediately starts to burn the Imitator. It melts rapidly and you are able to step away unharmed. Having no other choice, you somewhat apprehensively turn the handle of the other door. Turn to **262**.

304

There is a single Gold Piece lying in the bottom of the backpack. As you reach for it, you suddenly feel a light tickling movement on the back of your hand. You withdraw your hand slowly, trying to control your mounting panic, and are horrified to see a BLACK WIDOW SPIDER. Before you can shake it off, it sinks its poisonous fangs deep into your wrist. Lose 6 STAMINA points. If you are still alive, turn to **20**.

305

The tunnel ends at a flight of stone steps leading downwards. From the floor below you can hear the sound of barking dogs. Have you got an old bone with you? If you have, turn to **253**. If you have not, turn to **148**.

306

Before you can take a single step towards the Leprechauns, one of them throws some sparkling dust at you. You are immediately frozen to the spot, unable to move a muscle. You watch helplessly as the Leprechauns rummage through your backpack and run off with all your possessions, leaving your backpack empty. Lose 2 LUCK points. About an hour later the freezing effect of the dust wears off and feeling returns to your limbs. You are angry at your loss and stomp off north, determined to have your revenge. Turn to **29**.

307

The cupboard contains a wooden mallet and ten iron spikes, which you put in your backpack while wondering which door to open. If you wish to open the west door, turn to **263**. If you wish to open the north door, turn to **136**.

308

The Medusa shrieks as you enter her cage, keeping your eyes firmly closed and slashing your sword wildly from side to side. You feel the blade sink deep into her side and hear a loud thud as she slumps heavily to the ground. You open your eyes again and shudder at the sight of the prostrate figure of the Medusa. Her gown is fastened by a large brooch bearing a single bright red gem. It is a garnet, and you prise it out of its setting, put it in your pocket and leave the room to head north. Turn to **316**.

309

You scramble frantically around the floor in search of a pool of water, but do not find one. The acid burns with a searing pain deep down in your throat. Lose 3 STAMINA points. If you are still alive, *Test your Luck*. If you are Lucky, turn to **231**. If you are Unlucky, turn to **193**.

310

You reach the far wall of the chamber and see two doors. If you wish to open the door to your left, turn to **339**. If you wish to open the door to your right, turn to **262**.

311

The Barbarian reluctantly agrees to your alternative suggestion. You both step back and take running jumps over the pit. Landing safely on the other side, you continue down the tunnel. The Barbarian, who is leading the way, suddenly stumbles on a floor stone which tilts forward, triggering a boulder loosely set in the ceiling. It crashes down on top of him, knocking him to the floor and crushing his skull. You must continue your quest alone. Turn to 325.

312

The razor-sharp disc whistles past your head and bites deep into one of the pillars. Turning to face your would-be assassin, you prepare yourself as he advances, his long sword drawn.

NINJA   SKILL 11   STAMINA 9

If you win, turn to 232.

313

The tunnel ends at a junction. The footprints you have been following turn north and you decide to stay with them. Turn to 32.

314

Your sword cleaves the handle and, being separated from its parent body, you watch the membrane shrivel away and drop on to the floor. Having no other choice, you somewhat apprehensively turn the handle of the other door. Turn to 262.

315

The tunnel veers sharply to the left and comes to an end at a high wall in which there is a door. You hear a ferocious roar from the other side of the wall and you wonder what gargantuan beast could make such a noise. If you have a coil of rope and a grappling iron, turn to **129**. If you do not have these items, turn to **245**.

316

The tunnel continues for quite a distance before you reach a junction. If you wish to head west into the new tunnel, turn to **296**. If you would rather continue north, turn to **241**.

317

Tapping the side of the borehole with your sword, you tread your way blindly through the sticky slime. You follow its twisting and turning course for what seems an age and begin to wonder where it might lead. Suddenly you hear a slithering sound up ahead. You freeze with fear, your eyes desperately trying to pierce the pitch-black darkness. Before you realize what is happening, you are gripped round the neck by the powerful mandibles of another Rock Grub. It is the mate of the Rock Grub you killed and has been attracted by the smell of blood on your sword. It squeezes harder until your neck snaps like a small twig. Your adventure ends here.

318

After crossing the bridge, you run across the cavern floor. At last you see a tunnel in the far wall, which you race down until you reach its end at a heavy wooden door. The door is locked. If you have an iron key, turn to **86**. If you do not have a key, turn to **276**.

319

Your armour and sword weigh you down more than you think. In mid-air you realize with horror that you are not going to reach the other side of the pit. You crash into the side of the pit, some two metres below the rim, and tumble head over heels to the bottom. Turn to **285**.

320

You decide to search the Ninja and find a cloth bag in the folds of his robes. Inside it is a flask of water, some rice wrapped in a palm leaf, a jar of ointment and a beautiful diamond. Will you:

Eat the rice and drink the water?	Turn to **330**
Rub some of the ointment into your wounds?	Turn to **269**
Take only the diamond and leave the hall?	Turn to **127**

321

You pull the cord and watch the drape as it rises up the sides of an iron cage. The woman's voice urges you to be quick, telling you that the room is booby-trapped so that the floor will fall away in one minute because of your extra weight. If you still wish to help her, turn to **289**. If you would rather leave the room and head north up the tunnel, turn to **316**.

322

You pass the wooden chair and soon get back to the junction, turning right to head west. Turn to **43**.

323

After tying the rope around the rock, you lower yourself slowly to the bottom of the pit. Throm retrieves his rope by shaking it off the rock, and you set off together down the new tunnel. Turn to **194**.

324

Have you talked to the crippled servant of the Trialmasters? If you have, turn to **256**. If you have not, turn to **79**.

325

You stand up and carry on down the tunnel. Suddenly you see daylight at the end of the tunnel. You run forward towards the most beautiful sight you have seen for a long time, a clear blue sky and green trees. You walk as fast as you can towards the end of the tunnel and emerge expecting to see the welcoming sight of cheering people. But there is no hero's welcome from the people all around you. They are all dead. You are standing in a cold chamber littered with armoured skeletons and bodies. The exit to victory was just an illusion. Only the corpses of the past adventurers are real. Utterly dejected, you walk back towards the tunnel, but hit an invisible barrier. You are trapped in this ghoulish place and destined to end your days in the chamber of the dead.

326

Ahead you see that the tunnel turns sharply to the left. You turn the corner and almost bump straight into two fierce-looking ORCS, armed with morning stars and wearing leather armour. You are totally unprepared, and as you draw your sword, one of them swings its morning star at you. Roll one die. If you roll a 1 or 2, turn to **91**. If you roll a 3 or 4, turn to **189**. If you roll a 5 or 6, turn to **380**.

327

The Mirror Demon, being solely intent on grabbing your arm, makes no attempt to defend itself.

MIRROR DEMON   SKILL 10   STAMINA 10

If, during any Attack Round, the Mirror Demon's Attack Strength is greater than your own, turn to **8**. If you manage to defeat the Mirror Demon without it ever winning an Attack Round, turn to **92**.

328

You gaze round Ivy's room. Seeing a painting of another Troll hanging on the wall, you ask her if he is any relation. Suddenly her mood and expression change. She loosens her grip on you and smiles, saying, 'Oh yes. That is my dear beloved brother, Sourbelly. He has done very well for himself down south in Port Blacksand. He is now an Imperial Guard in Lord Azzur's elite troop. I'm very proud of him.' Ivy stares at the painting and continues to praise her brother. If you wish to slip out of the chamber through the door in the east wall, turn to **125**. If you would rather continue the conversation, turn to **99**.

329

You step up to the mirror and are amused by your distorted reflection. Your head looks as large as a pumpkin and your face is exceedingly strange. Suddenly, without warning, a terrible pain pounds through your head and you try to look away from the mirror, but you are unable to. Some evil force is keeping your eyes glued to your own reflection. You grip your head with your hands and realize with horror that it is expanding. You can withstand it no longer and, blacking out with the pain, you fall unconscious to the floor, never to wake.

330

The Ninja's rations are basic but welcome. Add 1 STAMINA point. If you have not done so already, you may either rub some of the ointment into your wounds – turn to **269** – or leave the hall, taking just the diamond – turn to **127**.

331

Touching the parchment has precisely the effect you had feared. The skeleton lurches forward and, rising from its chair in a series of jerky movements, raises its sword to strike you. Lunging sideways, you draw your sword to defend yourself.

SKELETON WARRIOR   SKILL 8   STAMINA 6

If you win, turn to **71**.

332

Your gem drops into the pool with a dull 'plop'. As you wait for something to happen, you start to feel faint. The gas rising from the pool is toxic, and you slump to the floor unconscious. *Test your Luck*. If you are Lucky, turn to **53**. If you are Unlucky, turn to **272**.

333

You hear footsteps and suddenly the trapdoor is thrown back. For a few seconds you are completely blinded by the bright light from the room above and do not see the Goblin thrusting his spear down-wards, or hear his sadistic laughter as the point pierces your neck. Your adventure ends here on the stone steps of the tunnel.

334

You try to wrench the tongue from your leg with your bare hands, but fail. Slowly you are dragged into the pool of slime, where you will be pre-digested and later consumed by the hideous Blood-beast.

335

Still running as fast as you can, you dive into the river. *Test your Luck*. If you are Lucky, turn to **67**. If you are Unlucky, turn to **101**.

336

The wristband was made and cursed by a Hag. It slows down your reactions and dulls your senses. Reduce your SKILL by 4 points. You kick the tunnel wall in anger and stomp off north. Turn to **298**.

337

The cool water is refreshing, but comes from a source which has been cursed by a Hag. Add 1 STAMINA point and lose 2 LUCK points. If you have not done so already, you may either drink from the other fountain – turn to **173** – or continue north – turn to **368**.

338

The bodies are those of two Orc guards. At least one of your rivals in the Trial of Champions must still be ahead of you. A quick search of the bodies produces nothing apart from a necklace of teeth hanging around the neck of one of the Orcs. If you wish to wear the necklace yourself, turn to **123**. If you would rather set off north without the necklace, turn to **282**.

339

As you touch the door handle, it goes soft in your hand, and when you try to pull your hand away, you find it is glued to the handle. A giant fist then forms in the centre of the door panel and shoots forward, punching you in the stomach. Lose 1 STAMINA point. If you have a jug of acid, turn to **303**. If you do not, turn to **236**.

340

Your fear gives you a new surge of energy and somehow your tired legs manage to keep you in front of the boulder. Ahead on your right you see the welcome sight of a doorway. You lunge at the door and mercifully it flies open. The boulder thunders past and you are left lying exhausted on the floor of a large room. Turn to **381**.

341

A crippled man with shackled feet shuffles into sight carrying a wooden tray laden with bread and water. He looks tired and miserable and, quite unmoved by the sight of you, tries to walk past. Will you:

Talk to him?	Turn to **367**
Take the bread and water off his tray?	Turn to **38**
Offer him some of your provisions (if you have any left)?	Turn to **169**

342

Your reactions are slow because of the poison in your system, and although you try to jump over the outstretched tongue, your legs will not lift you high enough. The sticky tongue wraps itself around your leg and starts pulling you towards the pool. You are dragged to the ground and are unable to unsheathe your sword. If you have a dagger, turn to **294**. If you do not have a dagger, turn to **334**.

343

In their twittering voices, the Troglodytes explain the rules of Run of the Arrow. They will shoot an arrow into the distance, and you will be allowed to walk unharmed to the point where it lands. However, you must walk barefoot, and you can see that the floor of the cavern is littered with sharp stones. As soon as you reach the arrow, the Troglodytes will start to chase you, and if they catch you, they will kill you. Suddenly one of the Troglodytes releases an arrow high into the air. It lands a long way away, and immediately the Troglodytes urge you to walk towards it. As you walk slowly towards the arrow, you hear the Troglodytes screaming excitedly behind you. On reaching the arrow, you look round to see the Troglodytes wave their arms in the air and set off after you. You start running as fast as you can, your feet bleeding from the cuts inflicted by the sharp stones and rocks. Lose 1 STAMINA point. Ahead you see an underground river running east to west across the cavern floor, with a wooden bridge crossing it. If you wish to run over the bridge, turn to **318**. If you wish to dive into the river, turn to **47**.

344

The tunnel twists and turns but keeps steadily north. Ahead you see a thin shaft of blue light streaming down from the ceiling to the floor. It sparkles and shimmers, and you can see images of laughing faces in the light. If you wish to walk through the light, turn to **229**. If you would rather walk round the light, turn to **107**.

345

You are about to enter the room when the Potion of Trap Detection begins to work and you are filled with a terrible premonition of danger. The room is set with a deadly trap. You decide not to go in and continue north along the tunnel. Turn to **252**.

346

You pull your boot off your foot and force yourself to reach up and hold it against the bell. Slowly the bell stops vibrating and the pain in your body gradually eases. You manage to stand up, but you do not release your boot from the bell until it becomes completely still. You put your boot back on your foot and then continue your journey west. Turn to **362**.

347

The Dwarf shakes his head, saying, 'All brawn and no brain is not enough to master the Trial of Champions. I regret you have failed. You will not be allowed to leave in case you impart its secrets to others. However, you have done well to get so far and I will appoint you my servant for the coming years to prepare the dungeon for its new contestants.'

348

You lunge at the Bloodbeast, trying to avoid the tongue which flicks out to grab your leg. Roll two dice. If the total is the same as or less than your SKILL, turn to **225**. If the total is greater than your SKILL, turn to **159**.

349

You lower yourself down the rope into the pit with one hand, using the other to grip your sword. The Pit Fiend is one of the most fearsome beasts you have ever seen, and you know this is to be one of the hardest fights of your life.

PIT FIEND   SKILL 12   STAMINA 15

If you win, turn to **258**.

350

The Giant Fly dives down and seizes you with four of its legs. It climbs quickly back to the roof of the cavern and you find yourself dangling helplessly in its grasp. Then, to your horror, it suddenly releases its grip and you fall ten metres to the floor, landing heavily. Roll one die and deduct the number from your STAMINA score. If you are still alive, you draw your sword just in time as the Giant Fly swoops down to try and recapture you. Turn to **39**.

351

The idol is very smooth and will be difficult to climb. Do you have any rope? If you do, turn to **396**. If you do not, turn to **186**.

352

Ahead you hear the sound of rocks being ground and crushed. The noise grows louder and suddenly you realize that the wall on your right is starting to collapse. Terrified, you watch as a large, hideous worm-like creature with a gaping mouth and extraordinarily powerful mandibles slithers through a hole in the wall. Its great jaws continue to crunch the rock as it turns its head slowly from side to side, feeling the cool air in the tunnel. It appears to be totally blind, but seems to know of your presence, perhaps sensing the heat of your body. It starts to slither towards you with its mandibles wide apart to attack. If you wish to fight the ROCK GRUB, turn to 254. If you would rather run back down the tunnel to the junction to head east, turn to 68.

353

Before you have time to get out of the way, the boulder smashes into your shoulder. Lose 1 SKILL point and 4 STAMINA points. If you are still alive, turn to 325.

354

The pill makes you feel as though the whole world is against you. Lose 2 LUCK points. The Dwarf tells you that you can now go on to the second stage of the test. He reaches for a wicker basket which, he informs you, contains a snake. He tips up the basket and the snake drops out on to the floor. It is a cobra and it rears up in the air, ready to strike. The Dwarf tells you that he wishes to test your reactions. You must grasp the cobra bare-handed below its head, avoiding its deadly fangs. You crouch down on the floor, tensing yourself for the moment at which to seize it. Roll two dice. If the total is the same as or less than your SKILL, turn to **55**. If the total is greater than your SKILL, turn to **202**.

355

You creep up behind the fighting Hobgoblins and, leaping out of the shadows, push them into the wall as you run by. You look back to see them sprawled on the floor and chuckle to yourself as you hurry on north. Turn to **110**.

356

There is an opening on the left-hand side of the tunnel wall. You are standing at the entrance of a large cavern, from which you hear a girl's voice crying for help. You can just make out the shape of a human figure rolling about on the floor at the back of the cavern. If you wish to enter the cavern and investigate, turn to **170**. If you would rather continue north along the tunnel, turn to **192**.

357

The Bloodbeast flops around awkwardly in its pool, and the smell of the poisonous fumes makes you retch as gas bubbles break the surface and contaminate the atmosphere. Will you:

Run round the side of its pool towards the tunnel?	Turn to **255**
Throw a gem into its pool (if you have one)?	Turn to **332**
Attack it with your sword?	Turn to **180**

358

You lose your balance and tumble headlong to the floor. Lose 2 STAMINA points. You decide against trying to climb the idol again, and run forward to the tunnel in the northern wall. Turn to **239**.

359

You fall off the rope and tumble head over heels into the chasm. You smash your head on a rocky outcrop, and by the time you hit the bottom of the chasm you are already dead.

360

After paying off the old man, you climb into the wicker basket and watch as he tilts his head back and shouts, 'Pull it up, Ivy!' The rope goes taut and the basket rises jerkily off the ground. As you are hauled higher and higher, the old man calls out to you, saying, 'You'll like Ivy, she's a nice girl. We call her Poison Ivy!' He starts to laugh uncontrollably and you wonder somewhat apprehensively just who is hauling you up. The basket goes through the ceiling and you find yourself in a small chamber, face to face with an ugly old female TROLL. Her face is hairy and covered with warts. With a huge hand she reaches forward and hauls you out of the basket, which she then lets fall to the floor below. She grabs you round the throat and says in a husky voice, 'I want paying too!' Will you:

Offer her something from your backpack?	Turn to **297**
Try to talk your way out of giving her anything?	Turn to **328**
Attack her with your sword?	Turn to **211**

361

The Pit Fiend's jaws snap at the monkey charm and pluck it out of the air. Suddenly its jaws spring open again, forced apart by the charm, which has expanded to fill its mouth. While the Pit Fiend thrashes around in the pit, trying to get rid of the charm, you lower yourself down into the pit to reach the double doors. In its mad rage, the Pit Fiend tries to crush you against the side of the wall with its massive body. *Test your Luck*. If you are Lucky, turn to **82**. If you are Unlucky, turn to **377**.

362

The tunnel veers sharply to the right and continues north for as far as you can see. You hear a tremendous commotion in the distance, growling and snarling and howling. You draw your sword and set off in the direction of the noise. Turn to **264**.

363

The food and drink are excellent, and you feel much better. Add 2 STAMINA points. Fully satisfied, you sit down and await the Dwarf's return. Turn to **302**.

As you are wiping the Manticore's blood from your sword, you are surprised to see a small man with a large nose suddenly jump out from behind one of the marble pillars. He is dressed in a tight-fitting green tunic and looks quite harmless, although you are wary of the way he is holding an opaque glass ball with a shimmering green light. 'Greetings,' he says cheerfully. 'My name is Igbut the Gnome, and I am the Trialmaster for your final test. Needless to say, my magical powers are great, so you should not try to attack me. You may have learnt during your quest that gems play an essential part in the Trial of Champions. The iron door in front of you is the victory exit, but there is only one way of opening it. Three gems have to be put into the lock mechanism, in a particular order, for the door to open. Each gem radiates a unique energy which will trigger the mechanism – if you do it correctly, that is. I will help you to a degree, but first we need the correct gems. Have you an emerald?' If you possess an emerald, turn to **31**. If you do not possess an emerald, turn to **3**.

365

You tell Throm that there is no point in killing the Dwarf as you will never find your way out of the chamber alone. You argue that an opportunity of tricking the Dwarf might arise later, once you have found the exit from the chamber, so you intend to go through with the Dwarf's test. You tell the Dwarf that you are ready and he beckons you to follow him, telling Throm to wait for his return. A secret door opens in the chamber wall and you follow the Dwarf into a small circular room. He closes the door behind you and hands you two bone dice, telling you to throw them on to the floor. You roll a six and a two: a total of eight. The Dwarf asks you to roll them again, but this time you must predict whether the total will be the same as, or less or more than eight. If you wish to guess that it will be the same, turn to **290**. If you wish to guess that it will total less than eight, turn to **191**. If you wish to guess that it will total more than eight, turn to **84**.

366

The temperature continues to rise steadily, far beyond the limits of human tolerance. Lying on the near-molten floor of the tunnel, you fail to regain consciousness. Your adventure ends here.

367

He looks at you warily when you tell him you are a contestant in the Trial of Champions. You ask him what he is doing in the tunnels, and he replies rather reluctantly that he is a servant of one of the Trialmasters, Baron Sukumvit's appointed controllers of sections of his dungeon. After chatting for a while, he admits that he would like to escape, but no one is allowed to leave the dungeon in case they reveal the secrets of its construction. He tells you that he hopes one day to bribe his way out, and that for one Gold Piece he will tell you where some treasure is hidden. If you wish to pay for the old man's advice, turn to **244**. If you would rather just wish him well and continue west, turn to **109**.

368

Leaning against the left-hand wall of the tunnel, you see a pair of bamboo stilts. They are securely chained, and you see a label attached to a padlock which reads: 'The price of these stilts is one Gold Piece. Place the coin in the slot to release the lock.' If you wish to buy the stilts, turn to **165**. If you would rather keep walking north, turn to **234**.

369

The tunnel turns sharply to the right, continuing east for as far as you can see. Throm stops and tells you to halt as well. He turns his head slowly from side to side, listening. 'I hear footsteps coming down the tunnel towards us,' he whispers. 'Draw your sword.' You both crouch down to hide in the shadows, and not a minute too soon, for a moment later you see the silhouette of two armed figures approaching. Throm jumps up and dashes forward, screaming a loud battle-cry. There are two CAVE TROLLS in front of you. Throm attacks the first one with his battleaxe, and you run to his aid and attack the second Cave Troll.

CAVE TROLL   SKILL 10   STAMINA 11

If you win, turn to **288**.

370

As you run round the side of the pool, the Bloodbeast flicks out its long tongue once again. Roll two dice. If the total is the same as or less than your SKILL score, turn to **104**. If the total is greater than your SKILL score, turn to **342**.

371

You take aim and hurl the wooden ball at the skull. Roll two dice. If the number rolled is the same as or less than your SKILL score, turn to **273**. If the number rolled is greater than your SKILL score, turn to **113**.

372

You finally reach the warrior's body, but as soon as you touch the jewel, both it and the warrior vanish into thin air. You hear the door slam behind you, followed by a sudden ominous rumbling above you. You look up and see the ceiling start to lower. You run to the door to try to escape, but it is locked and there is no handle on the inside. The ceiling gradually drops, until you are forced to lie on the ground, trying to halt the ceiling's progress with your hands and feet. But it is a hopeless task, and you are crushed to death in the stone vice.

373

You clamber on to the soft boulder, half expecting to be engulfed by it at any moment. Getting over it is difficult, as your limbs sink into its soft casing, but eventually you manage to struggle over it. Relieved to be back on firm ground, you head east. Turn to **13**.

374

You walk around the cavern, but find nothing of interest. Throm calls out behind you, saying that he has found a leather pouch under a pile of rocks. Opening the pouch he laughs out loud as a tiny mouse runs through his fingers and scurries off into a crevice between two boulders. Suddenly you hear the sound of cracking rock above you, and look up to see stalactites breaking off the roof. Throm's booming laugh, which still echoes through the chamber, has made the stalactites vibrate and break off. You yell at Throm to run through the archway as the stalactites start to crash to the floor. *Test your Luck*. If you are Lucky, turn to **118**. If you are Unlucky, turn to **295**.

375

Acrid smoke rises from the jug as you lower the cloth into it. The liquid is unmistakably acid. You recork the jug and place it in your backpack, hoping it may be of use later. You sheathe your sword and press on northwards. Turn to **110**.

376

The Gnome, still smiling, says excitedly, 'Excellent! Just one to go. Do you possess a diamond?' If you have found a diamond, turn to **62**. If you have not found a diamond, turn to **3**.

377

The huge beast slams its body against your arm, and you lose your grip on the rope. Crying out in pain, you tumble to the bottom of the pit. Lose 5 STAMINA points. If you are still alive, turn to **203**.

378

Somewhat nervously, you take a deep breath and dive into the dark pool. The northern wall does not project very far beneath the surface of the water, and you decide to take the risk and swim under it. You soon start gasping for air, and are forced to swim upwards. You try not to think that you may be trapped in an old submerged tunnel and are very relieved when you surface into cool air. You are on the other side of the wall, and can see the tunnel rising out of the water and continuing north into the distance. You wade out of the water and check the contents of your wet backpack. *Test your Luck*. If you are Lucky, turn to **112**. If you are Unlucky, turn to **209**.

379

Exhausted by your long duel, you fall to your knees. As you stare at Throm's still body, a bitter loathing for the Dwarf fills your heart. Somehow you will avenge Throm. Engulfed in your hatred, you do not notice the Dwarf enter the arena until he is standing right in front of you, a loaded crossbow aimed at your chest. 'I know what you are thinking,' he says

calmly, 'but remember that only I know the way out of here. Get up, it's time for you to leave.' Once on your feet, the Dwarf indicates that you should walk ahead of him. Back in the chamber, he crosses over to the northern wall and pushes against one of its stones. A door-like section of the wall swings out, opening into another crystal-lit tunnel. With his crossbow still aimed at your chest, the Dwarf smiles, saying, 'Good luck.' If you wish to walk straight into the tunnel, turn to **213**. If you would rather take a punch at the Dwarf, turn to **145**.

380

The Orc's morning star crashes into your shield and bounces off harmlessly. The tunnel is too narrow for both of them to attack you at once, so you are able to fight them one at a time.

	SKILL	STAMINA
First ORC	5	5
Second ORC	6	4

If you win, turn to **257**.

381

You look round the room and see nothing of interest apart from an alcove in the west wall and a stone chair in the middle of the room. Sitting in the chair is the skeleton of an armed warrior, possibly a contestant from years gone by. The skeletal fingers of its right hand are gripped round a piece of parchment. If you wish to take the parchment from the skeleton, turn to **331**. If you would rather walk over to the alcove, turn to **128**.

382

The old man points at one of the statues, and you recognize it immediately. It is the knight who started the Trial of Champions, the agonized look on his face locked in stone for eternity. The old man smiles, saying, 'This man weighs 100 pounds plus half his weight. How much does he weigh?' What will you answer?

100 pounds?	Turn to **144**
150 pounds?	Turn to **227**
200 pounds?	Turn to **391**

383

Much to your surprise, nothing extraordinary happens to you while you are sitting in the chair. There is nothing else to do but continue north up the tunnel. Turn to **188**.

384

The fourth step suddenly gives way under your weight. Your leg sinks into a deep hole, and before you have time to pull it out, you feel a pain in your foot as unseen sharp teeth sink into it. The high-pitched squeaking you hear below is being made by rats. They are starved, and rip into your foot, hungry for your flesh. Lose 2 STAMINA points. You regain your balance and manage to pull your leg out of the hole. Three rats are still hanging on to your foot with their teeth. Kicking frantically, you smash their heads against the banister until they let go. You then wrap crude bandages torn from your shirt around your bleeding foot and climb the steps to set off north again. Turn to **277**.

385

You pour the contents of the glass phial into your mouth and swallow the clear liquid. Although you do not feel any immediate change, you hope that the potion will create the illusion that you are a TROGLODYTE just like the ones in front of you. Taking a deep breath, you step boldly into the cavern. The Troglodytes continue their tribal dance, believing you to be one of them. You walk past them casually and head north. Unfortunately, the effects of the potion are short-lived. Suddenly you hear a shriek behind you as one of the Troglodytes spots you, and you are forced to run across the cavern floor. Ahead you see an underground river running east to west through the cavern and a wooden bridge crossing over it. If you wish to run over the bridge, turn to **318**. If you wish to dive into the river, turn to **47**.

386

You walk no more than three metres west before you hit an invisible barrier. It starts fizzing and crackling, and you are thrown back. You have hit an energy screen. Lose 1 STAMINA point. There is no alternative but to walk back to the junction and head north. Turn to **218**.

387

Ahead you hear the thud of heavy footsteps approaching. Out of the gloom steps a large, primitive being dressed in animal hide and carrying a stone club. On seeing you, he grunts and spits on the floor, then raises his club and lumbers on towards you, looking anything but friendly. You draw your sword and prepare to fight the CAVEMAN.

CAVEMAN   SKILL 7   STAMINA 7

If you win, turn to **114**.

388

The tunnel soon comes to a dead end. A piece of paper, brown and curled with age, is pinned to the end wall. If you wish to pull it off the wall to see whether there is a message written on it, turn to **23**. If you would rather hurry back down the tunnel to join the Barbarian, turn to **154**.

389

Without your weapons you are more vulnerable, and the loss of your sword leaves you feeling almost naked. Lose 4 SKILL points. Wondering whether you have made the right decision, you follow the tunnel north. Turn to **181**.

390

You crouch down beside the plinth below the cross-bows' line of fire. You reach up and pull the skull off the plinth, expecting your action to trigger off the crossbows. Much to your surprise, nothing happens. Add 1 LUCK point. Still crouching, you pluck the jewelled eyes out of the skull. You recognize the yellow stones as topaz, and place them in your backpack. Looking at the row of crossbows, you wonder whether a trap still awaits you in this room. Will you:

Crawl out of the room holding the skull?	Turn to **15**
Replace the skull on the plinth before crawling out of the room?	Turn to **204**

391

Still smiling, the old man looks at you and says, 'Well done, Stranger. You have answered correctly. I wish you good fortune during the rest of the Trial of Champions, and, to this end, I shall increase your powers.' He then mutters a few more unintelligible words and you feel a powerful surge soar through your body. Add 1 to each of your SKILL, STAMINA and LUCK scores. You bid the old man farewell and leave his room to continue north along the passage. Turn to **100**.

392

You just have time to hear the Gnome say, 'Three skulls', before a white bolt of energy shoots out from the lock into your chest, knocking you unconscious. Roll one die, add 1 to the number and reduce your STAMINA by the total. If you are still alive, you come to and are told by the Gnome to try again. You didn't get any of the gems right, so you won't try that combination again.

A	B	C	
Emerald	Diamond	Sapphire	Turn to **16**
Diamond	Sapphire	Emerald	Turn to **392**
Sapphire	Emerald	Diamond	Turn to **177**
Emerald	Sapphire	Diamond	Turn to **287**
Diamond	Emerald	Sapphire	Turn to **132**
Sapphire	Diamond	Emerald	Turn to **249**

393

You enter a cold room divided by a deep chasm. A rope is stretched taut across the chasm to the far side, where a magnificent winged helmet rests on top of a pole. If you wish to walk across the tightrope to reach the helmet, turn to **274**. If you would rather return to the tunnel to continue north, turn to **291**.

394

You smash the glass with the hilt of your sword, making a hole big enough to climb through. Immediately the Giant Insects start swarming and jumping towards you. Wasting no time, you clamber into the room, grabbing one of the lit torches to defend yourself. The fire keeps most of the Insects at bay, but by the time you have snatched the crown and climbed back into the corridor, some will certainly have stung you. Roll one die and add 2 to the total. This is the number of stings you have suffered and you must reduce your STAMINA by 1 for each sting. The Giant Insects do not chase you, preferring the bright light of the room they are in. You examine the crown, and see with disgust that it is merely painted iron, and the 'diamond' is just glass and totally worthless. You throw it on the ground in a rage and wonder which way to go next. If you wish to head west, turn to **59**. If you would rather return to the junction to head north, turn to **14**.

395

On hearing the noise of your scabbard, one of the
Troglodytes raises the alarm. You stand up and run
as fast as you can through the cavern. One of their
bowmen lets fly an arrow as you run. It pierces your
shoulder with deadly accuracy. Lose 3 STAMINA
points. If you are still alive, turn to **259**.

396

You make the rope into a lasso, whirl it above your
head and throw it at the idol's head, smiling happily
as it falls around its neck. You then tighten the
noose and start to climb, hauling yourself up the
rope. You are soon at the top of the idol, sitting on
the bridge of its nose and holding on to the rope.
You draw your sword and wonder which jewelled
eye to prise out first. If you wish to prise out the left
eye, turn to **151**. If you wish to prise out the right
eye, turn to **34**.

397

The liquid is a magical potion which will enable you to detect hidden traps. Add 2 LUCK points. If you have not done so already, you may open the red book – turn to **52** , otherwise, you must continue north with Throm – turn to **369**.

398

Although you cannot see any visible trap, you have a strong feeling that the chest contains a hidden danger. The Potion of Trap Detection is working well. You stand to one side of the chest and lift the lid with your sword, holding it at arm's length. As the lid rises, an iron ball hanging on a cord swings back and breaks a glass capsule fixed inside the lid, instantly releasing a gas. Fortunately, you have time to jump back without inhaling the poisonous fumes. Once the gas has cleared, you walk back to the chest and look inside it. There is a pendant chain lying in the bottom, but somebody has taken the stone from its setting. You feel so annoyed that you throw the chain on to the floor and storm out of the room up the tunnel. Turn to **230**.

399

The bread contains secret elven healing herbs. Add 3 STAMINA points. Feeling sad yet strong, you pack away the mirror and the charm and leave the cavern to head north. Turn to **192**.

400

As soon as you appear at the tunnel exit, a large crowd of people begins to cheer and shout. You walk down a path lined with jubilant people towards a small rostrum, and there, sitting under a colourful bamboo umbrella, is Baron Sukumvit. He looks astonished, as if he never expected anybody to come through his Deathtrap Dungeon alive. Now the secret of Fang is known. As the Baron rises from his chair, you climb the steps to the rostrum, bow down before him and watch as his cold eyes stare at you in utter disbelief. You smile grimly as he offers you his outstretched hand. To the deafening noise of the cheering people of Fang, Baron Sukumvit opens the chest containing your prize of 10,000 Gold Pieces. Then he places a laurel crown on your head and proclaims you the Champion of Deathtrap Dungeon.

1.   THE WARLOCK OF FIRETOP MOUNTAIN
Steve Jackson and Ian Livingstone

Deep in the caverns beneath the threatening crags of Firetop Mountain, a powerful Warlock lives, guarding a mass of treasure – or so the rumour goes. Several adventurers like yourself have set off for Firetop Mountain, but none has returned. Do you dare to follow them? Who knows what terrors you may find!

2.   THE FOREST OF DOOM
Ian Livingstone

Only the foolhardy would risk an encounter with the unknown perils that lurk in the murky depths of Darkwood Forest. Yet there is no alternative, for your quest is a desperate race against time to find the missing pieces of the legendary Hammer of Stonebridge – fashioned by Dwarfs to protect the villagers of Stonebridge against their ancient doom.

3.   THE CITADEL OF CHAOS
Steve Jackson

You are the star pupil of the Grand Wizard of Yore and your mission is to venture into the dark, doom-laden tower of the demi-sorcerer, Balthus Dire. Risking death at every turn of the passage, will you be able to overcome the six-headed Hydra, the peril of the Rhino-man and the deadly and mysterious Ganjees? With only your sword and your magical skills to aid you, your task is truly awesome.

4. STARSHIP TRAVELLER
Steve Jackson

Sucked through the appalling nightmare of the Seltsian Void, the starship Traveller emerges at the other side of the black hole into an unknown universe. YOU are the captain of the Traveller and her fate lies in your hands. Will you be able to discover the way back to Earth from the alien peoples and planets you encounter, or will you and your crew be doomed to roam uncharted space forever?

5. CITY OF THIEVES
Ian Livingstone

Terror stalks the night as Zanbar Bone and his bloodthirsty Moon Dogs hold the prosperous town of Silverton to ransom. YOU are an adventurer, and the merchants of Silverton turn to you in their hour of need. Your mission takes you along dark, twisting streets where thieves, vagabonds and creatures of the night lie in wait to trap the unwary traveller.

7. ISLAND OF THE LIZARD KING
Ian Livingstone

Kidnapped by a vicious race of Lizard Men from Fire Island, the young men of Oyster Bay face a grim future of slavery, starvation and a lingering death. Their master will be the mad and dangerous Lizard King, who holds sway over his land of mutants by the strange powers of black magic and voodoo. Will you risk all in an attempt to save the prisoners?

FIGHTING FANTASY

Steve Jackson

The world of Fighting Fantasy, peopled by Orcs, dragons, zombies and vampires, has captured the imagination of millions of readers world-wide. Thrilling adventures of sword and sorcery come to life in the Fighting Fantasy Gamebooks, where the reader is the hero, dicing with death and demons in search of villains, treasure or freedom.

Now YOU can create your own Fighting Fantasy adventures and send your friends off on dangerous missions! In this clearly written handbook, Steve Jackson has put together everything you need to become a successful GamesMaster. There are hints on devising challenging combats, monsters to use, tricks and tactics, as well as two mini-adventures complete with GamesMaster's notes for you to start with. The ideal introduction to the fast-growing world of role-playing games, and literally countless adventures.